# The Black Stallion's Filly

"She'll never make a racehorse," the crowd said when Black Minx was led into the sales ring.

*Let the others see only her faults,* thought Henry Dailey, the trainer. And he bought the filly and took her home to Alec Ramsay. "With her blood she'll run," Henry predicted.

But little did Henry or Alec dream what was ahead of them. Black Minx had a mind of her own, and she put them to tests they'd never experienced before. They even had to fashion a false tail for her to wear!

This fast-paced story takes you to the exciting preparatory races that lead to the Kentucky Derby—and finally to the great classic itself.

*All titles available in both paperback
and hardcover editions*

# The Black Stallion's Filly

### by WALTER FARLEY

RANDOM HOUSE · NEW YORK

Library of Congress Cataloging in Publication Data

Farley, Walter
The black stallion's filly
New York, Random House [1952]
1. Title      PZ10.3.F22Bme      52-7216
ISBN: 0-394-80608-5 (trade hardcover)
      0-394-90608-X (library binding)
      0-394-83916-1 (trade paperback)

*For Paula Turner,*
*who first read this book as a young girl,*
*and whose dream came true*

# Contents

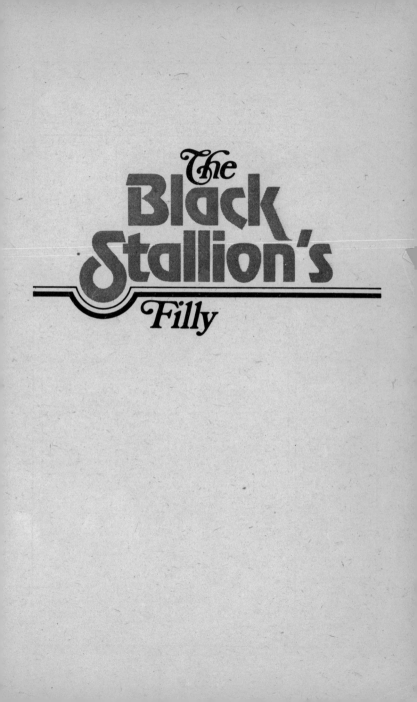

The Black Stallion's Filly

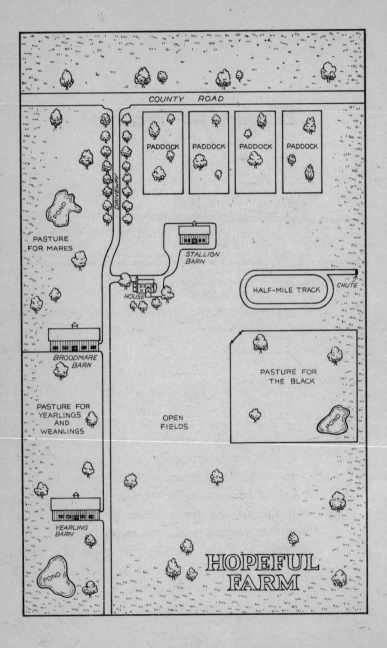

# *Hopeful Farm*

# 1

The following sports column written by Jim Neville appeared in newspapers throughout the United States on November 14.

### Farewell, Satan

This is an obituary. There are two reasons why you read it here rather than in the special section which this newspaper devotes to the deceased. Number one, my subject is a horse. Number two, he isn't dead yet.

But for me and the millions of others whose sole contact with our racing thoroughbreds is at the track he's as good as dead. For once a racehorse leaves us to spend the rest of his life in retirement at a stock

3

farm he's gone forever as far as we're concerned. Certainly we think of him again whenever his sons and daughters appear on the track for the first time. But his colts and fillies are distinct individuals in themselves and we look upon them as such. Never do we say with any degree of honesty, *"Here he is again!"*

So it was with sincere sympathy and sadness that we watchéd Satan step onto the Belmont Park track yesterday for his last look around before being shipped home to Hopeful Farm in permanent retirement.

Satan, sired by the Black, had a racing career that was much too short for one who had so much speed yet to give. He was unbeaten at two, three and four years of age, winning some of our greatest classics. Last season he lost only one race, the San Carlos Handicap at Santa Anita Park, California, in December. He ran that race, we learned later, with a stone pounded deep inside his right forefoot. Yet he wouldn't quit. Although he was running on only three legs it took a photo finish for Night Wind to beat him to the wire in race record time!

X-ray photographs taken after the race disclosed a fractured sesamoid, one of the small bones in the ankle. The injured leg was put in a cast and Satan was shipped home. We were sure that he had reached the end of his

racing career. But during the spring en-
couraging reports reached us. The injured
leg had healed and Henry Dailey was putting Satan back in training. By summer the
burly black horse was stabled at Belmont
Park, and during his works he looked as
powerful as we all remembered him. But
Henry Dailey wasn't satisfied. He took Satan
along slowly, never asking too much of him,
never quite ready to race him. Only last
month did Henry step up Satan's works.
And then the great horse went sore again in
the injured leg. Last week it was decided that
to prevent further injury Satan would be re-
tired permanently.

Yesterday, at the insistence of the track
management, Satan took his last look
around Belmont Park—the scene of so many
of his brilliant wins. And for the thousands
who packed the stands, it was a sad but
thrilling moment when he came out of the
paddock gate between the seventh and
eighth races.

The weight of a rider might have aggra-
vated his injury at this time, so he was led
out by Henry Dailey, riding Hopeful Farm's
gray stable pony, Napoleon. As Satan
pranced there was no evidence of the leg injury that had brought his racing days to an
end. He stepped lightly and a little faster at
the crowd's first and most thunderous ova-

tion. He looked very beautiful and very gay with black and white ribbons braided into his mane. He was the picture of health and energy. That he could look as he did and yet be able to race no more accounted for the wealth of feeling which moved so deeply all who watched him.

As Henry Dailey led him up the track to the far turn and then back down past the stands again, the track announcer told of Satan's achievements. But I don't believe anyone really listened. They knew all there was to know about Satan. They listened only to the beat of his hoofs as he loped beside Napoleon. And they most probably remembered—as I did—his hard-driving, blazing stretch runs down this very same track in other years.

He stood perfectly still while they took pictures of him near the paddock gate and the track band played "Auld Lang Syne." His black body glistened in waves of supple muscle. Neither the photographers, the shouts from the crowd, nor anything else bothered him or caused him to move one step from Napoleon's side. He was the picture of everything a well-trained racehorse should be.

I noticed that his hardened old trainer, Henry Dailey, blew his nose countless times. But I don't think Henry had a cold any more than I did, and I was blowing my nose too.

Finally, Satan was led away and the applause of the crowd moved with him. His last curtain call was over. For me and for most of those who have been privileged to watch him race he is gone forever.

Farewell, Satan.

At Hopeful Farm, Alec Ramsay put down the newspaper. He carefully clipped the sports column, placing it in the center of the huge desk before him. Henry would want to keep it in Satan's bulging scrapbook. Season after season Henry had carefully and wisely trained and raced Satan. Time and time again he had said that Satan was the greatest horse ever to set foot on any track. The world had said so, too. And Henry had cut pictures and stories of Satan from countless newspapers and magazines. He had made Satan a champion who stood majestically on top of the world—and Henry had been right up there with him.

Now it was over. Satan was coming home. Henry was coming home.

"But it's not the end for Satan at all," Alec said to himself. "It's just the beginning, really. He'll sire colts and fillies as great as he was."

Rising from the deep-cushioned chair behind the desk, Alec walked to the window. As he crossed the room, numerous objects hanging on the walls of the office caught his eye. They were bronze plaques which had been awarded to Satan in years past. The great horse had showed his heels to the best animals on the track. None of them could hold a candle to him. None could outstay him. None could outsprint him.

Maybe Satan would be glad to quit the track, to forget forever the chunks of earth flying in his face, blinding him as he made his move from behind the front runners. Maybe so. But how about Henry? Could he give it all up, even for a short time?

At the window Alec looked out upon the large empty paddocks between the stallion barn and the county road. The morning sun was unusually hot for the middle of November, and he could feel its warmth through the glass. He opened the window, then strode across the office and went out the door.

He stood in the wide corridor of the stallion barn. He sniffed deeply the scents he loved, the smells of well-oiled leather and soap and hay and manure. He listened to the sound of the Black rustling his straw. Finally Alec moved again, walking past the light and airy box stalls, all empty save one.

He stopped before the end stall. The heavy oak door was closed but he could see the Black through the iron-barred windows. Quickly Alec opened the door and went inside the stall.

This was the boss, the great sire of Satan. The stallion stood in the rays of the sun which came through the large top window to the rear of his stall; his black coat caught and reflected the brightness of the morning.

"Hi, fellow," Alec said. "Let's go outside."

The Black stood with his head high in an attitude of conscious grandeur. But then he neighed and pushed his nose into Alec's chest with the playfulness of a very young colt.

The boy scratched the soft muzzle, even pulled the long tongue whenever it emerged from the stallion's mouth. It was one of the games they played.

As Alec snapped the lead shank to the halter, he spoke softly. "They're coming back today. Satan and Napoleon and Henry. It's going to be like old times again."

The stallion pulled against the lead shank, anxious to leave his stall. Alec didn't keep him waiting. They moved quickly onto the wooden floor of the barn's entryway and then out through the end door into the sunshine.

Going past the paddocks toward the Black's own field a quarter of a mile away, Alec kept the stallion at a walk. Yet the boy was constantly aware of the flicking of the small ears, the burst of energy that would explode like a giant firecracker the moment he turned the Black loose in the field. Alec continued talking to him but never forcing him. Ask him nicely and the Black would do what he wanted. Try to push him around or force him and it would be all off. There never had been a battle of wills between him and the Black; there never would be.

The half-mile training track lay directly ahead of them, and Alec led the stallion to the fenced field to the right of it. Here the Black had ten acres for his very own. Reaching the fence gate, Alec opened it. There was no holding the stallion now; all he wanted was to be set free.

"Easy, boy. Easy," Alec said, turning him loose.

The Black lunged and bolted across the field, his head held high, his body stretched out with tail fanning the wind. Alec watched him until he disappeared down the hillside.

*Even Satan couldn't match* his *speed,* he said to himself, *now or ever.*

But no one knew, not even Henry. The Black had raced just once, long ago. Most people had forgotten him just as they'd forget Satan in time. Next year there would be another horse which would win the acclaim of racegoers and newspapers and magazines. But here, at Hopeful Farm, life would go on pretty much as always for the Black and himself, for the mares and foals.

Alec returned to the stallion barn but didn't go inside. Instead he stood before it, his gaze moving to the three mares in the rolling pasture across the driveway. They were all in foal to the Black and in the months to come might produce a colt or a filly as great as he had been.

Beyond the broodmare barn was still another fenced field and in the distance he could see the mares' three weanlings at play. All were colts. Next January they'd be yearlings, and the following year they would be preparing to race as two-year-olds. Henry would be most happy then, for he would have complete charge of their training. But what would Henry do between now and then with no Satan to race? He could perform endless chores on the farm but he wouldn't be happy away from the track. He had spent too many years training to be content taking care of the mares and their youngsters.

The great rumbling of a truck interrupted Alec's thoughts. It was coming along in the distance, its ponderous size claiming the county road for its very own. Alec smiled when he saw it. Nothing but the best for Satan, he thought. Henry had hired a six-horse van to bring Satan and Napoleon home.

Alec started for the paddock gate. He knew that Henry would have the van stop there. And Satan would be allowed to run for a while to get the kinks out of his legs after his trip.

The van turned carefully into the driveway, its high roof striking the branches of the low-hanging trees which grew on either side. As it came closer, Alec could make out the faces of the two men in the cab and he knew that Henry, as always, was back in the van with his horses. Finally the truck came to a stop. The top half of the side door was already open and Henry's white head emerged as he shouted directions to the drivers. He waved to Alec, then disappeared within.

The two men left the cab to help Alec lower the wooden gangplank from the door of the van to the ground.

"Easy trip?" Alec asked them.

"Never easy with Henry," one said. "He treats his horses better than their own mothers would. But we're used to him by now."

"He won't let us go over thirty at any time," the other said. "An' we always have to hog the road, riding the crown, so as not to jostle 'em."

The first man nodded in agreement. "Anyone tryin' to pass us always has a job. But Henry don't care how mad they get just so long as his horses ride easy."

Henry appeared in the doorway holding Napoleon by the halter. His eyes were fixed on the heavy fiber mat which lay on the ramp. "Y'sure you got that mat tight? I don't want any slipping."

"It's fast. We checked it twice," one of the drivers said patiently.

"Alec, you better check it. Make sure."

"Okay, Henry."

"Now come up and take Napoleon down."

"Yes, Henry."

Moving up the ramp, Alec took the gray horse by the halter and rubbed his muzzle. "Hi, boy," he said. "It's good to see you."

Henry stood on the other side of Napoleon. He wore his battered hat and his brow was wet with sweat. "You take him to the second paddock, then come back an' help me with Satan."

Alec smiled. "You take it easy now, Henry. You're home. Everything is all right."

Henry's gray eyes, still so very worried, met his young friend's for the first time. "I just don't want him to hurt himself getting down."

"He won't and you know it. You never saw a horse so easy to load and unload as Satan."

Henry's gaze dropped. "Yeah," he said. "But get along with you now."

Fat and well groomed, but his back sagging with old age, Napoleon whinnied as Alec led him through the van's door. His hoofs came down on the matting calmly and deliberately, his step like that of an old gentleman leaving his favorite club. He whinnied again when he saw the familiar paddocks and barns, and moved a little faster.

When Alec returned to the van, Henry had Satan in the doorway.

"Alec, you check that mat again. Napoleon might have loosened it some."

Resignedly the two men stepped away from the ramp while Alec went over it again. "It's fast, Henry," he said finally.

Satan stood quietly at Henry's side with only his large eyes showing any evidence of his excitement at being home. His fiery gaze followed Napoleon as the gray horse moved ponderously about the second paddock.

Henry was talking to Satan, moving him onto the ramp. The horse never hesitated. He walked as carefully, as deliberately, as had Napoleon.

Henry wiped his wrinkled brow when he had Satan safely on the ground, then he turned to the two men. "Slim," he said, "you an' Harry stick around a few more minutes before you go. I want you two up at the far end of the paddock when I set him loose. I want you to wave him down if he works up too much speed. Don't let him run into the fence an' hurt himself."

"Sure, Henry," one driver said, shrugging his shoulders. "We got time since you're payin' for it."

When the men had left for the far end of the paddock, Henry turned to Alec. "You and I will stay at this end. We can't be too careful, y'know."

"No, we can't," Alec agreed. He knew Satan was well able to take care of himself in the paddock but he couldn't smile—not with Henry's eyes, full of concern, boring into his own.

A few minutes later, Henry led the great champion through the paddock gate and set him free.

"You get down the fence a piece," Henry told Alec. "Don't let him hurt himself."

Alec moved along the fence, watching Satan as he galloped up the field. The horse was stretching out but had full control of himself. Satan was smart enough not to run into any fence even though it was his first outdoor frolic in a long while. It would take only a few minutes for him to become accustomed to freedom again. Alec saw the two men at the far end of the pasture raise their hands, waving down Satan as he neared the fence. The horse turned and came back, snorting joyously at Napoleon in the next paddock.

Alec watched Satan in full gallop. As the horse neared, the boy raised his hand a little, more to pacify Henry than to keep the horse from running into the fence. Satan went past, galloped across to Henry, then went up the paddock again.

Alec's eyes continued to follow him, but now he was comparing Satan with his sire.

*His head is much heavier and larger than the Black's. He pushes it out when he's galloping, while the Black 'most always runs with a high head. Satan's neck is shorter and more muscular. And his body is so heavy that it gives you the feeling of grossness. But when he stretches out, as he's doing now, you forget his great bulk and see only the beauty of his coordination. He's like the Black in many ways, but very different in others.*

A short while later, when Satan had settled down and was moving quietly about the paddock, Henry let the drivers go. Now he stood beside Alec at the fence, just watching his horse.

"It's not Satan I'm worried about," Alec said after a while. "I know he's glad to be back. But what are *you* going to be like—without a horse to get ready for next season's races?"

"You don't need to worry about me none."

Alec tried to catch his friend's eye. But Henry kept following Satan's every movement.

"Are you going to be happy helping me around here?" Alec asked.

"Sure."

"I'm not so sure," Alec said. "You're not much of a stock-farm man."

"I got Satan to look after."

"But it won't be the same for you. You won't be getting him ready for any races."

"No, I won't," Henry said glumly. He glanced quickly toward the far pasture where the weanlings played, then back to Satan. "By this time next year I'll start getting those fellows ready."

"But in the meantime?" Alec asked.

Henry shifted his weight against the fence, then pushed himself upright with a thrust of his shoulder. "Would you think I was nuts if I told you I wanted to buy a horse to race next spring?"

Alec smiled. "No, I wouldn't. It's more what I expected you to say." He paused, running his hand around the collar of his tight turtleneck sweater. "We've got the farm paid off, and all the bills for the new barns, the fencing, and the training track have been paid. Dad showed me the books the other night. We don't owe anybody, and there's enough money left over for running expenses and for buying another horse if you know of a good one, Henry."

The trainer pushed back his hat. "No, I wasn't figuring it that way, Alec. I don't want to use the farm's money. We'll need every cent of it to pay expenses for the next couple of years. If Satan was racing, we wouldn't have to worry about a thing. But since he isn't we got to be careful about every penny we spend."

"Then what are you driving at, Henry?"

"I got a little money saved. I thought I'd go to the Kentucky fall sales next week and maybe find a horse I like at a price I can afford to pay. Maybe I'll be lucky and get a good one. But I don't want to take a chance with the farm's money—not with all the broodmares we still need to buy before we get a good band together. I'll do this on my own or not at all."

"Go ahead then, Henry, if that's what you want to do." Alec was watching Satan stretch his head across the fence. "Do you have any particular horse in mind?"

"No, I guess not. They'll probably all go too high for me. If I want 'em, so will somebody else with more money to spend. Still, there's one I just might . . ." Henry stopped. His gaze was on Satan too, but he was not following the horse's movements.

"Yes?"

"Remember our first few months here, long before we had any mares of our own?"

"Sure, Henry."

"Do you remember a mare by the name of Elf, sent to us by a Doctor Chandler of Lexington, Kentucky? She was bred to the Black."

"A dark-brown mare on the small side," Alec answered. "She always came out of the barn on her toes. Yet she was level-headed; nothing upset her, not even the Black. She was a big little mare."

"You remember good," Henry said.

"It's our business to remember," Alec replied.

"I liked her a lot."

"I know. You wanted to buy her, but her owner wouldn't sell." Alec turned to Henry. "You thought," he continued, "that combining her quiet disposition with the Black's high spirit might produce a very fine horse."

*"Maybe it has,"* Henry said quietly.

Their gazes met.

"What did Elf have?" Alec asked.

"A filly that's two years old now."

"Then she's the Black's first daughter," Alec said quietly. "All the others have been colts." He turned away from Henry to look in the direction of the training track. He couldn't see the stallion in the field beyond. "I wonder what she's like?" he added, more to himself than to Henry.

"I don't know. I never saw her. But she's up for sale next week. I came across her name in the catalogue."

"What's her name?"

"Black Minx. And I got a feeling I'll like what I see," Henry said. "I sure liked her dam, and with the Black as her sire . . ."

Again their gazes met and held.

"I hope you get her, Henry," Alec said. "I've got sort of a feeling about her too."

Nothing more was said. Each understood the other so well. Each knew that something good might come of their mutual interest in a filly they had never seen, a filly named *Black Minx*.

# *The November Sales*

## 2

For four days Henry had sat in the very seat he now occupied in the indoor sales pavilion near Lexington, Kentucky. He had watched the auctioneer's gavel fall 498 times as 256 yearlings, 51 broodmares, 68 weanlings and 123 older horses had been sold to the highest bidders. There were 33 more horses yet to enter the ring, including Black Minx, before the fall sales would be concluded.

There came a moment's respite from the sing-song chant of the auctioneer as another yearling was sold and led from the ring. Henry sat back in his seat, the wicker chair creaking beneath the weight of his heavy, stocky frame. He pulled down his hat a little more over his eyes. He wanted as few people as possible to recognize him. This would not be easy, for he knew most of the five hundred or more who packed the big room.

He'd been here often in the years past, long before he ever

knew Alec and the Black and Satan. But it had been different then. As a trainer he'd come along with his various employers. He'd spent their money. Or rather he had told them when to bid and when not to bid, depending on how much he liked the looks of a horse and what he thought to be a fair price.

But this time he was bidding *his* money for *his* horse. Although he had trained hundreds of racehorses, he never had owned one in his life. Funny. Well, that was the way it went with some people. He had to admit he was pretty excited about buying his own horse. That was funny too after all these years.

The amount of money in his pocket was pitifully small, considering what everyone else had been paying for horses at this sale. Four colts had already been sold for more than fifty thousand dollars. So far he'd seen ten two-year-olds he'd have liked to own, and he'd bid his thousand dollars each time. But they had been sold for far above that figure. The colts he'd wanted were wanted by other people too, but those people had more money to spend. Well, he'd known this would happen. He had told Alec it would.

His thoughts returned to Black Minx. She'd be stepping into the ring in about an hour or so. Alec had told him to use some of the farm's money if she went over what he could afford on his own. Maybe he would, if he saw a chance of getting her.

The room became unusually quiet. Henry glanced at his catalogue, and knew the reason for the almost reverent hush. What was supposed to be the top yearling of the sale would be the next to enter the sales ring.

With a flourish suggestive of unheard trumpets heralding

his approach, a tall gray colt was led out. The auctioneer went to work over the public-address system.

"Now, folks, you all listen to me," he told the crowd. "Heah we have what could be the finest colt in this sale. He's by Mahmoud, out of Cry Baby, and that makes him, as you all know without mah tellin' you, a full brother to Silver Jet!" He paused a moment to let the full impact of his words sink into the crowd. Then, "And you all know that Silver Jet stood in this very same ring last fall as a yearling . . . just like this colt is doin' . . . and went away from heah the property of Tom Flint to win for that gentleman the grand and mighty sum of more than one hundred and eighty-five thousand dollars this year as a two-year-old! There's no better investment for your money than something like that. Am I right, Carl?"

The auctioneer turned to his assistant, who, taking the cue, said into the microphone, "You're dead right, Jim. And, folks, I'll let you in on a little secret which you all know. Tom Flint bought Silver Jet in this ring last year for only ten thousand dollars! But you're not going to get this heah full brother for no ten thousand dollars. No, sir! Too many folks right heah know Silver Jet won more money than any other two-year-old colt this year. Too many folks right heah know Silver Jet is the colt to beat in the Kentucky Derby next May! And you all know that this colt is his full brother. And you all want him. But in order to get him, folks, you're going to open up your wallets. Yes, sir, *this colt may be the one*! And I see Tom Flint in that back row, just sittin' on the edge of his chair and waitin'. He's got Silver Jet and now he's out to get this heah fine-looking full brother. All right, Jim. Heah we go! Sell him!"

The auctioneer took over the microphone and the pavilion resounded to his musical sing-song chant as he got his first bid of fifteen thousand dollars.

"I'm bid fifteen, fifteen, fifteen. Who'll go twenty, twenty? I got twenty, twenty, twenty. Make it thirty, thirty. *Yeah!* I got thirty, thirty, thirty. Make it forty, forty. I got five, five, five, thirty-five. Make it forty, forty, forty. *Yeah!* I got forty, forty, forty. I want fifty, fifty, fifty. I got fifty, fifty. I want sixty, sixty, sixty. I got five, five, fifty-five. I want sixty, sixty, sixty. I got eight, eight, fifty-eight. Make it sixty, sixty, sixty. I got nine, nine, nine, fifty-nine. Make it sixty, sixty, sixty. I want sixty, sixty, sixty. *Yeah!* I got sixty, sixty. Make it five, five, sixty-five. I want five, five, sixty-five. I got two, two, sixty-two. I want five, five, sixty-five, five, five, sixty-five. I want five, five, sixty-five. I want five, five, sixty-five, five, five, sixty-five. Make it five, five, sixty-five, five, five, sixty-five. I want five, five, sixty-five, five, five, sixty-five." Suddenly he stopped.

For a moment the pavilion was quiet. Then the auctioneer said, "Now listen heah, folks. You all know that sixty-two thousand dollars isn't much to bid for this heah colt." Although he spoke to more than five hundred people, his words were meant for the two bidders who alone remained in competition for the gray colt.

Now he singled out one of them—a man sitting near the sales ring—when he said, "Mr. Ashwood, you're not going to let Mr. Flint get this heah colt, are you? You went up to sixty thousand dollars. Will you make it sixty-three thousand? That's not too much money for this colt. Silver Jet came home with more than one hundred eighty-five thousand dollars this year for Mr. Flint. You're not going to let him take his full brother too, are you?"

The man near the ring shifted uneasily in his seat but didn't offer a bid over Flint's sixty-two thousand dollars. Yet the auctioneer didn't think he'd lost him so he decided to wait a few more moments. He knew Tom Flint would go still higher to get this colt. All he had to do was to get another rise in bid from Ashwood. So he would wait a few minutes before closing the sale in order to give Ashwood a chance to think it over and to realize that he wanted this colt enough to pay sixty-three thousand dollars for him.

The auctioneer's gaze moved to the right of Tom Flint. In a corner chair he saw the short, bulky figure of a man whose hat was pulled down almost completely over his eyes. The auctioneer didn't recognize him but watched as the man drew a handkerchief from his pocket and blew his nose. The harsh sound of it broke the strained stillness of the pavilion.

Smiling, the auctioneer said, "The gentleman back theah. Did you just make a bid for this colt?"

Henry pushed back his hat. "No," he grunted. "I just blew my nose."

Only then did the auctioneer and the crowd recognize Henry Dailey, and the room rocked with laughter.

"Well, Henry," the auctioneer said, "you'd better be careful how you blow your nose or you'll own this heah colt." But then his attention and that of the crowd was diverted to the man seated near the ring. Mr. Ashwood was holding up three fingers.

Once again the auctioneer's chant claimed the pavilion. "I got three, three, sixty-three. I want five, five, sixty-five." He was looking at Tom Flint now, and after a few seconds Flint held up four fingers.

"I got four, four, sixty-four." He turned to Mr. Ashwood. "I want five, five, sixty-five."

The bidder nodded without taking his eyes from the gray colt in the ring.

"*Yeah!* I got five, five, sixty-five. I want six, six, sixty-six." Back to Tom Flint in the last row. ". . . six, six, sixty-six." Flint nodded. "*Yeah!* I got six, six, sixty-six."

Once more the auctioneer's gaze swept to Mr. Ashwood. "Give me seven, seven, sixty-seven."

This time the man near the ring turned to his right and spoke to his trainer. A moment later, Ashwood swept his hand across his chest and shook his head. He was finished and would bid no higher.

The auctioneer's eyes traveled once more over the crowd, looking for a bidder who might keep this colt in the ring to bring a still higher price. "All done?" he asked. "Are you all done at sixty-six?" His intent gaze became fixed on Henry Dailey. "How about you, Henry? Here's a colt to take Satan's place in your stable."

Henry shook his head, not bothering to raise his hat from his eyes. Never would he pay sixty-six thousand dollars for this gray colt, even if he'd been spending someone else's money. No unbroken, untried yearling was worth that much, regardless of pedigree. Tom Flint should have known better than to go so high for this colt.

Henry heard the fall of the auctioneer's gavel and the words, "Sold to Tom Flint for sixty-six thousand dollars."

Raising his hat, Henry saw the gray colt leave the ring. Well, that's that, he thought. As far back as he could remember, it was the highest price paid for a yearling at a public sale. He noticed the sudden restlessness of the crowd.

Many of the men were on their feet and moving toward the exits. Good, he thought, let 'em go. The fewer people here the better. He had known the sale of the gray colt would be the highlight of this session. He had counted on some of the crowd leaving afterward. It was part of his plan to get Black Minx at a price he could afford to pay.

Henry turned to the windows. The weather was lending him a helping hand, too. It had turned cold yesterday, and this morning it had rained. During the afternoon the rain had turned to snow that was now falling heavily. The pavilion was five miles from the hotels in downtown Lexington. Driving conditions wouldn't be good, and those who remained in the pavilion were starting to worry about getting back at all. They thumbed the pages of their catalogues, trying to decide whether or not it was worth their while to stay until the end of the session.

"Get along, folks," Henry muttered. "Get along with you." More people left within the next few minutes, and the empty chairs in the pavilion were more than he had dared hope to find.

A broodmare, heavy with foal, was in the ring. The assistant auctioneer was giving her pedigree hurriedly in an attempt to arouse the interest of the prospective buyers who had started to leave. "Here's a grand mare for any stock farm," he said. "She's by Count Fleet. She's the dam of the stakes winner, Bewildered. And the foal she's carrying is by Bull Lea. You couldn't possibly go wrong in . . ."

The snow came down more heavily, taking more people from the room within the next fifteen minutes.

Henry was smiling beneath the cover of his hat when he felt a large hand on his knee and heard the creaking of the wicker chair beside him as someone sat down. Looking up, he saw Tom Flint's large, beefy frame; then his gaze went higher to the man's jovial face and wide-brimmed hat.

"Can I give you a lift into town, Henry?" Flint asked.

"No, Tom. But thanks. I think I'll stick around a little longer."

Tom Flint consulted his catalogue. "Interested in something coming up?"

"Guess not. Just don't have anything else much to do." He kept his gaze on his folded hands. He felt that to meet the Texan's gaze would be to shout to him that he was going to get Black Minx if he could. His way of buying was to look only at the auctioneer, never at a competitor, and this he practiced now.

"They made me go pretty high for that gray colt," Flint said.

"Too high. You shoulda known better, Tom." He sincerely liked this big, robust man. Flint was wealthy, but unlike most owners he trained his own horses. He didn't hire someone else to do all the work and then sit on the sidelines until it was time to collect the trophies. He was at the track morning after morning, doing the real work, the dirty work. When a good prospect went lame or sour, Flint wept with his swipes and exercise boys. And when he had something, like his Silver Jet this year, he had the satisfaction of knowing he'd done his share of work in developing the colt. No, there weren't many owners left like Tom Flint.

"I couldn't let that yearling brother get away from me, Henry. Not with Silver Jet racing like he is."

"Most often full brothers let you down," Henry said quietly. "We expect too much from 'em."

"Yeah, I guess so. But I'm out to win the Kentucky Derby, Henry. If Silver Jet doesn't win it next May, maybe this colt will do it for me the following year."

Henry was silent until Flint asked, "How are things at Hopeful Farm?"

"Fine. Just fine." He wanted Flint to go. The auctioneer was selling the remaining horses fast because of the weather and the few people left in the pavilion. Soon Black Minx would enter the ring. Henry didn't want any competition from Tom Flint.

"It's too bad, Henry, that you didn't buy a farm in this area rather than in New York State. Even with your having stallions like the Black and Satan, an owner of broodmares thinks twice before sending them that distance from here. You should have settled in Kentucky and made it easy for everybody to get to your stallions."

"Alec picked out the farm," Henry said. "They're his horses. We'll make out all right."

"I never see Alec at the races any more."

"No, he takes care of things at the farm. He prefers it to the track."

"Yet how that guy can ride," Tom Flint said heartily. "I remember the ride he gave the Black years ago in Chicago. Nothing I've seen since has equaled it."

"I know," Henry said, his eyes remaining on the auctioneer. A three-year-old colt was being sold. The next one in the ring would be Black Minx and Tom Flint was still here. Henry tried not to betray his nervousness. He pulled his hat down farther over his eyes.

"Well, I guess I'll be going," Flint said.

*Go ahead then! Go!* Henry heard the shifting of Flint's

frame in the wicker chair; then the man was on his feet.

"You're sure I can't give you a lift to town? It's nasty out."

"No, thanks. I'll get a lift later." He didn't want Flint to know that he was driving the farm's small van, hoping to take home Black Minx. "So long, Tom," he said.

But Flint didn't go. He remained there beside him. The auctioneer's gavel was ready to fall, ending the sale of the three-year-old colt. It would be only a matter of a few minutes now before the filly would enter the sales ring.

"So long, Henry." Flint took a step away; then he stopped again. "This two-year-old filly by the Black . . ." he began.

Henry didn't lift his eyes. He didn't move. He just waited.

"I saw her first start in Florida last February," Flint added. "She was pretty bad."

That was all he said. But Henry realized that Flint hadn't been fooled, that Flint had known all along why he was waiting. Henry looked up then and saw the big man leaving the pavilion; he just wasn't interested in the filly.

Black Minx came into the ring held firmly by the white-coated attendant who handled all horses up for sale. She was coal black and small. She had a quick, competent walk as she was led about the ring, and it was apparent to Henry that her limited size was misleading, for she had more muscle than was noticeable at first glance. Her head was light and beautiful with great breadth between sharp eyes, a slightly dished nose, a narrow muzzle, and sensitive nostrils. Her only disfigurement was a short tail, so short that it was barely more than a stump.

It was not the first Henry had seen of Black Minx. He had visited her in the sales barns behind the pavilion, but his visits had been few. He was afraid that his interest in this black filly would get around. Disclosing only mild interest in her, he'd talked to her groom and others who had been close to her.

"She's erratic and temperamental," they had said.

*That's the Black in her,* he'd decided for himself, for he had liked the filly at first sight.

"She's apt to fly into tantrums at the drop of a hat, either in play or in anger," Henry had been told. "She bites."

*That's the result of poor handling, poor training. She's been spoiled.*

"She'll never make a racer."

*With her blood she'll run, if I can get it out of her.*

Henry clenched his hands. Let the others remember only her faults. Let the others discard her as Flint had done. He would have a good chance then of taking her home. The money in his pocket burned his leg. Now, as he watched the filly, he wanted her more than ever.

The assistant auctioneer was giving Black Minx's pedigree. "This two-year-old filly is by the Black, folks, and I don't need to remind you that he's the sire of Satan, champion at two, three, and four years of age. And her dam is Elf, an unraced mare because of an early leg injury. Now you all know that this heah filly is the property of Mrs. David Chandler and that her husband, Doctor Chandler, had one of the finest stock farms in this section up until his death two years ago. Mrs. Chandler sold all racing stock at that time except for this heah filly. You won't find a better-looking two-year-old, folks. She's ready to be raced. She might be the one! Don't you think so, Jim?"

"I do, Carl. I most certainly do," the auctioneer said into

the microphone. "And heah we go! Heah we go! Who'll start the bidding off for this real fine filly?" His anxious eyes went quickly over the small number of people remaining in the pavilion. "She might be the three-year-old we'll all heah about next season! Yes, sireee! Heah we go! Who'll say a thousand dollars for her?"

Henry's eyes stayed on the auctioneer, yet his ears were alert for any bid. If they started at a thousand dollars, he wouldn't stand a chance of getting her. He waited, a little afraid even to breathe. A bid came, but it wasn't the thousand dollars asked.

The auctioneer accepted it. "I got five hundred, five, five. Make it a thousand. I'm asking one, one . . ."

Henry relaxed a little. The low bid as a starter made it plain to him that the people left weren't going up very high to get this filly. They were afraid of her. Maybe they thought they knew too much about her. Well, he knew all they did and, in addition, he saw something more. He'd use all his money and, if necessary, some of Alec's to get her.

His eyes shifted from the auctioneer to the filly, who pawed often and pulled the attendant about the ring. Not once did Henry look at the other people in the pavilion. But he knew their number was small, and he gave thanks again to the heavy snow.

Within the next ten minutes two more bids were made for Black Minx. But they were raises of only a hundred dollars each time. Henry knew the auctioneer was becoming vexed and impatient with the low and slow bidding.

Suddenly the sing-song chant stopped and the room was quiet until the auctioneer said angrily, "Folks, seven hundred dollars isn't a fair price for this heah filly! You're all wrong, dead wrong. She's worth ten times what you've bid on bloodlines alone, even if you never race her. She's a good filly, a fine filly. You're all making a mistake heah, a *big* mistake. Now let's open up our wallets. Heah we go!"

But before he could begin his chant, a man sitting almost directly below him said quietly but loudly enough to be heard throughout the pavilion, "Jim, you're wastin' our time as well as yours. Most of us heah know this filly as well as you do since she was foaled and raised only a couple of miles away. And we know there's a lot more to tell about her than what you've been shoutin' at us from up theah. So you'd better just sell her for what you got now and get on with the other horses. I for one want to get home before we're all snowed in."

The auctioneer was silent for a moment, and his face showed that he was furious at the interruption. "All right, Bill," he said at last, "if that's the way you want it. But you all listen to me for one more second about this heah filly. Those of us left are mostly homefolks, born and raised right around these parts. We were all good friends of Doc Chandler. We all know what kind of horses he bred. This heah filly is one of them. And I maintain, in spite of what you all think you know, that someone is going to make monkeys out of all you with this heah filly." He paused. "Now, boys, for the last time do I heah any bids higher than seven hundred dollars?"

Henry pushed back his hat. The time had come for him to get the auctioneer's attention. He nodded and raised one finger and his lips moved to say one thousand. He hoped a boost of three hundred dollars over the last bid for the filly would discourage anyone else from bidding and would close the sale of Black Minx.

It did just that. The gavel fell on the board as the auctioneer said, "Sold to Henry Dailey for one thousand dollars. In my opinion he just got the best buy of this heah sale."

Henry slumped in his seat. It had been a hard, nerve-wracking four days. Now to get his filly home to Alec—*his filly!*

# *Home Again*

## 3

Alec's alarm sounded at five o'clock, as it did on every morning of the year. Turning it off, he rolled quickly off his back and sat on the side of the bed, his hands supporting his head. Not that he enjoyed rising so quickly at the first burst of the alarm. No, not at all; but he knew it was the only way. To lie in bed, even for a moment, was to fall asleep again, and too many horses were waiting to be fed.

He seemed sleepier than usual this morning, as he looked out the window into the darkness. He would be glad to see the long days of summer again, and awaken once more to the light. It always seemed easier then.

Alec had on his sweatshirt and overalls, and was putting on his boots when he remembered. No wonder he was so sleepy! Henry and the filly had arrived shortly after midnight. He had heard the van and gone to help unload. He had been too drowsy to notice much, and now he was too sleepy to remember anything at all about the new filly. It would take him a little time. The ammoniated smells of the barns would clear everything up; they always did.

Leaving his room, Alec stumbled down the narrow, winding stairs of the old stone house, and entered the living room with its hand-hewn beams stretched across the ceiling. He passed through a door into the kitchen of the modern one-story addition his family had built. Because his mother and father were asleep in their bedroom at the end of the hall, Alec moved quietly. In the dining room he pushed the thermostat higher. A large picture window was directly opposite him, and during the day he could look out upon the paddocks and pastures. But in this early-morning darkness he couldn't see a thing. He couldn't tell if it was snowing again or not.

Going to a closet, Alec put on his jacket and got a flashlight. Then he went out the door. It wasn't very cold; a breeze swept his face, promising rain rather than snow. The ground was soft beneath his feet and his boots made deep sucking noises in the mud as he walked toward the stallion barn. The snow of a few days ago had completely disappeared. He would turn the horses out later in the morning if it didn't rain. Mud wouldn't hurt them any. But a cold rain falling on their backs at the same time would invite any number of illnesses.

The Black, Satan, and Napoleon greeted Alec in unison when he entered the stallion barn and switched on the lights. He stopped to take three great breaths. Sure enough, his head cleared with the smells of the barn, and he felt more wide awake. He threw down a few bales of hay from the loft above. Then he went down the line, first to Satan, then to

Napoleon, and then to the Black in the end stall. As he pitched the hay on the floor for each horse, he thought again of Henry, who had insisted on tearing out the overhead hay racks.

"Feed the hay on the stall floor," Henry had said. "It's natural for a horse to graze with his head down. That way you keep any dust from gettin' into his eyes and nose. Sure we'll waste some hay. But it'll be worth it."

Alec freshened the water in each stall trough, and then fed the grain. He had learned so much from Henry. Everything they had here was the result of Henry's guidance and help. Without him Hopeful Farm never would have existed.

Alec stood beside the Black, watching him blow into his feedbox while he ate. "Did you know you have a daughter?" he asked. "She's here. She came last night." The stallion didn't raise his head from the box; he was much too busy eating.

A moment later Alec left the stallion barn. The broodmares, the weanlings and the new filly were waiting for him. His flashlight bobbed along as he cut across the field to the weanling barn. The filly had been put in the broodmare barn. He'd get to her, along with the mares, after feeding the weanlings.

Alec grinned as he thought of Henry and his filly. Two nights ago, right after Henry had bought her, he'd phoned from Kentucky. He'd sounded like a kid who had bought his first horse. Well, wasn't that just about it? And the next day Henry had started for home, driving steadily for more than twenty-four hours before he and the filly had arrived last night. He'd been worn out and looked it. His eyes had been terribly bloodshot; his white hair had seemed even whiter. But his enthusiasm for the filly hadn't been dampened by the long, arduous drive from Kentucky. He would have spent hours talking about her if Alec hadn't made him go to bed in his apartment over the broodmare barn.

All Alec could remember about the filly was that she was small and didn't seem to have any tail. But he could be mistaken. Soon he would know everything about her.

Reaching the weanling barn, he went through the same feeding and watering routine he had followed in the stallion barn. He hurried a little, for he knew that the broodmares were most likely nickering impatiently and might awaken Henry. His friend needed all the sleep he could get this morning.

Alec ran most of the quarter-mile which separated the two barns. When he had almost reached the broodmare barn, the lights went on; he knew Henry was up. Going inside, Alec found him pitching hay to the mares.

"Why didn't you stay in bed?" Alec asked a little angrily. "You need more rest."

"Couldn't sleep any longer. Anyway, I don't require much."

Henry's hair was tousled and his face crusted with sleep. He had taken time only to pull on his clothes before coming downstairs.

Alec said, "I'll finish up the mares. Go see your filly."

Henry grunted. "Okay," he said, and hurried down the end corridor to the other side of the barn where they had put Black Minx.

After Alec had run fresh water for the mares, he gave them their hay and grain for the morning. A shrill neigh came from the filly. Henry would take care of her, all right;

he would treat her like a princess. Already she had one of the largest stalls on the farm—a foaling stall—for Henry had insisted that she be given plenty of room to move about after her long trip.

Finishing with the mares, Alec joined Henry. He found him standing outside the filly's stall door. As the two friends moved along together, Alec watched the Black's first daughter. He noticed first that she wasn't touching her feed. She just stood there, her black body tense and expectant, her small head turned toward them with sharp eyes, inquisitive and waiting.

"Why isn't she taking her feed?" Alec asked.

Henry's gaze didn't leave the filly. "Her groom at the sale told me that when she gets excited the only way to get her to eat is to feed her out of your hand."

It wasn't necessary for Alec to ask Henry if the filly was excited now. Everything about her indicated it. "How long has this been going on?"

"The hand-feeding?" Henry asked. Without waiting for a reply, he added, "Since she was a foal."

"No, I meant her excitement."

"She's been excited ever since the sale, but she'll get no hand-feeding from me. She's been spoiled long enough. She'll eat out of her box or not at all." Henry paused. "She'll get to it eventually. She did on the trip up."

Black Minx moved a little closer to them, pushing out her muzzle.

"She has a lovely head, Henry," Alec said. "It's small and well shaped, like the Black's."

Henry nodded. "She's a big little filly," he said with a sudden rush of eagerness. "Not at all as small as she looks. See how deep and well sloped her shoulders are, Alec. And her withers couldn't be better. Look at her hindquarters, too—big and strong." Henry was pointing now, his hand extended over the stall door. "She's well ribbed up in the middle, too, and those legs of hers are just as clean and shapely as I like to see 'em. She'll go a distance. Mark my words, Alec. She'll be more than a sprinter, a lot more!"

Alec saw the filly's muzzle move. "Careful, Henry!"

But he was too late. Black Minx had nipped and torn Henry's shirt.

They stepped back while Henry pulled up his sleeve. There were no teeth marks. She hadn't caught his flesh.

"My fault for not watching what I was doing," Henry grumbled. "She tried it a couple of times on the trip, too, but I was always ready for her."

"She doesn't look mean," Alec said.

"She's not. She just doesn't know any better."

"What do you mean, Henry?"

"Well, here's the story I got on her. This filly was only a weanling when old Doc Chandler died. His widow sold all their stock, but she kept Elf as a saddle mare for herself. She gave the filly to her young grandchildren as a pet. And a pet is exactly what they made out of her. The kids—they were about high-school age—taught her what they thought were cute tricks. Stuff like gettin' her to rear and paw the air at them, and sometimes to put her forelegs on their shoulders while they walked in front of her. Then, too, they always had her lookin' for carrots and sugar in their pockets. She'd pull away at their clothes, and they'd laugh about how she had such a time finding what they had for her."

Henry stopped because Black Minx had moved to her

feedbox and was whiffing her grain; finally she began to eat. "See, Alec," he said. "You just got to have patience and wait for her. We'll make her a real good-mannered lady one of these days."

For several more minutes Henry watched the filly before continuing his story. "Anyway, Alec, the Chandler kids thought all those tricks were pretty funny at first. But when she started growing up and getting stronger the tricks weren't so funny any more.

"They kept away from her when she started rearing and pawing the air at them. They stopped carrying tidbits in their pockets. Her hoofs and teeth were big and strong, for she was a yearling now, and she could hurt when she played or went after carrots and sugar in their pockets. The kids didn't want to play any longer but she couldn't get that into her head. She'd played too long with them to stop all of a sudden."

Henry gestured at the filly's hindquarters. "That docked tail, for instance. Let me tell you how she got it."

Alec's eyes were on the pitiful little chewed-off tail that was most unlike the filly's sire's.

"There's no doubt that the filly, as a yearling, was hard to handle and very mischievous. But it wasn't her fault she'd got that way. Whenever the kids entered the paddock in front of her barn she'd run after them, probably thinking of the game of tag they'd taught her. But now the kids were scared and ran, and most often, I guess, they got real angry with her. Anyway, one day she caught one of the boys and nipped him, taking off some of his sweater and some of the skin off his back. As I heard it, he was more mad than hurt. So a few minutes later when he saw the filly going into her stall at the end of the paddock, he ran after her and slammed the door hard to keep her penned up. The heavy door caught her tail, and when the vet came he had to amputate most of it."

Alec's face was grim. He said nothing when Henry concluded with, "So that's the way it's gone for this little filly. No wonder she bites and paws. But I know I'll be able to do something about both. It'll just take time and patience."

After a while Alec pushed himself away from the stall door. "Did the Chandler kids keep her after the accident to her tail?" he asked.

"They left the picture," Henry said, "by going to college, and Mrs. Chandler turned the filly over to a trainer to be raced as a two-year-old. But she picked a guy with a big stable, who was never able to give the filly all the time she needed after what she'd gone through. He took her along with his stable to Florida last February and started her in one race."

"What'd she do?"

"Swerved across the track before she reached the first turn, and went through the rail. It took twenty-nine stitches in her breast to put her back together again. The jockey, Nino Nella, got a fractured collarbone out of it."

"You sure got yourself a filly," Alec said grimly.

Henry turned to him, and Alec noticed the dark circles beneath his eyes. Yet when he spoke his tone was sharp, even a little defiant. "Do you think, Alec, that I could have got this filly for a thousand dollars otherwise? No, sir. No one else at the sale wanted to take the time with her. They all got too many horses to go to all the bother of makin' over a spoiled one. But I got the time. And I know something else. She's got the blood and the body and the spirit to make a classic horse." He paused, smiling now. "Do I look as though I'm taking a real deep plunge having such high hopes for this filly?"

Alec's face lightened too. "You look as if you think you are," he said. "You look as though you find it more exciting than comfortable."

"Maybe so," Henry said, turning back to his filly. "But this little girl and I are going out to win the Derby. We're going to . . ."

"You're going to *what?*" Alec couldn't keep the astonishment from his voice.

Henry just repeated, "The Derby, Alec. We're going out to win the Kentucky Derby."

When Alec spoke again he had regained full control of his voice. "It's almost December," he said calmly, "and in five months, by the first week in May, you're going to have rid this filly of her bad manners and have her trained and ready to go *a mile and a quarter?*"

"I'm going to try, Alec," Henry said.

Alec turned away. "Come on, Henry. Mom has breakfast all ready by this time. You need some good strong coffee."

But Henry didn't move from the stall door. "I'll be there in a little while, Alec. I want to groom her down good when she's finished eating."

Alec turned back. Henry wasn't looking at him; he had eyes only for his black filly.

It was light when Alec left the barn. His brow was puckered, his thinking confused. What Henry planned to do with Black Minx was fantastic, incredible. With her background, faults, and lack of training, how could Henry possibly think of her even as a Derby *starter*? And even if he was miraculously lucky and got her to the post, what possessed him to think she might win? From the running of the first Kentucky Derby in 1875 until now, *only one filly* had won the great classic, and that was Regret, back in 1915. Fillies just didn't win the Derby. They just couldn't beat good colts over that grueling distance of a mile and a quarter so early in the spring of their third year. Countless record-breaking fillies had tried it, only to be licked in that last hard furlong. Yet Henry had said, *"We're going out to win the Kentucky Derby."*

Alec pushed his red hair off his forehead. He hated to think that Henry, after all his years of experience, was letting his emotions carry him away. No, it couldn't be that, Alec decided. He wouldn't let himself even think it. Instead he went back in memory to the days when Henry had taken him and the Black under his wing, when Henry had encouraged him to race the Black because he had confidence in Alec's ability to handle the stallion on the track.

At the time Henry's enthusiasm had sounded just as fantastic as what he'd said a few moments ago. But it had turned out the way Henry had said it would. He had ridden the Black to victory over the two best horses in the country.

Then Satan had come along. Alec hadn't thought it possible for any horse ever to approach the Black's blinding speed. But Henry had looked at the weanling Satan and said, "This colt might make you change your mind, Alec."

Fantastic again *at the time*. But Satan's race records now proved how right Henry had been.

Alec stopped in front of the house. He wanted to clarify his thinking before going inside.

If Henry had said he was going to get Black Minx ready for the Kentucky Derby, he'd do just that. It didn't mean necessarily that she'd win, but it did mean that she would be trained for that classic in early May. She would be ready to go the full mile and a quarter.

Alec decided that during the months to come he would never again question Henry's ability to reach his goal. Instead he would help Henry with his filly in every way possible—just as Henry had helped him with the Black and Satan.

Alec continued up the walk, ready now for a good breakfast.

# The Reluctant Filly

## 4

For Alec it was like old times having Henry around every day. That week, the last in November, they exercised Satan and the Black. Together they handled weanlings and broodmares, and performed routine farm chores. Henry was his former cheerful self because he had a coming three-year-old to get ready for the following spring and summer campaigns. Alec laughed more, too. He found that, after all, he had not divorced himself completely from the lure of the racetrack; he could still be excited by the schooling of a young racehorse.

He watched Henry with the black filly, taking a keen interest in each step of her progress. He marveled again at Henry's unlimited patience that had done so much to win his reputation as one of the finest colt trainers in the country.

"Just give me a break in the weather and I'll have her

ready," Henry said over and over. "An easy winter, so I can get her out on the track 'most every day, is all I ask."

The weather was mild that week, but Black Minx didn't set foot on the training track. Instead Henry kept her in the barn, and he got to know her ways pretty well.

Alec noticed that Henry was all business when he entered her stall, which was often. Never did he fondle her or play, as Alec might have been tempted to do. Henry went about his work with the unconcern of a man accustomed to handling horses—with the least amount of fuss or outward exertion. He was gentle but firm with the filly, and always on the alert for any bold move she might make toward him. Only his hand would reach out when it came; one sharp slap on muzzle or foreleg was his reprimand.

Alec had no idea how many times a day Henry groomed Black Minx that first week. Lots, anyway. Her body shone like glossy satin from soft sponges, soft brushes, soft cloths. But Henry wasn't at all interested in bringing out the beautiful luster of her black coat. Rather it was his way of teaching her good manners.

"We're just getting acquainted now," he had told Alec the first day he spent with her. "No more hand-feeding, and for the present a lot of grooming. That may be all we'll have to do to stop her nipping. I don't know. But we'll start there, anyway."

The filly had stood tied very short with a soft cotton rope around her neck and through her halter.

"I watched the groom getting her ready at the sale," Henry had continued. "He made the mistake most people make with a filly like this, and that probably goes for the trainer who took her to Florida. He gave her too much freedom of head, and when she turned on him he tried to straighten her out by a blow with his brush or towel. The trouble was he usually missed. So it all became a game to her, like everything else. I keep her tied short. I want her to learn I mean business. But at the same time I want to make my grooming a pleasure for her, so I use nothing but soft cloths and the like. She's thin-skinned and ticklish. Never should she be given a real hard going-over."

It was the first of December when Henry took Black Minx out of the barn. She stood in the cool and brisk morning air with her highly polished body brilliantly reflecting the sun's rays. Her first week of stall schooling was over. She was ready for a little freedom. But she wouldn't be allowed to romp for hours on end as did the mares, weanlings, stallions, and even old Napoleon. No, she would be given just a short time to frolic alone. Then Henry's hand would be on her halter again. She was different from the others; her goal was the Kentucky Derby only five months away. Her days would be spent under saddle, jogging, galloping, and breezing. Always she would feel the weight of a rider on her back, his hands on her mouth. She would know no other life for a long, long time to come.

Henry's hand moved against the filly's head, shifting her balance so she was always in motion and couldn't collect herself to rear or paw. He had led her about inside the barn many times during the past few days. She tried fewer tricks now than she had at first. Still he had to be very careful, never giving her a chance to think of anything but what he wanted her to do. He turned to Alec, standing a short distance from them.

"Did you put Satan in the barn?" he asked.

"Yes," Alec replied, "and Napoleon is in his paddock, as you wanted."

"How about the Black?"

"He's in his field," Alec said. "It's a nice morning and I only put him out there a short while ago. He needs the exercise."

"I guess it'll be all right. He's probably at the far end of the field, isn't he?"

Alec nodded, but his eyes were on the filly. Henry had stopped moving her in those small circles. Alec waited to see what she'd do. Sure enough, her foreleg came up and she pawed the air. Henry brought the end of the lead shank smartly against her leg.

"Mind!" he said firmly. "Stand still."

Alec knew that she had not struck out viciously. She had done it more in play. But it would not have been much fun for anyone to have been on the receiving end of such a blow.

Henry was moving her again. "One good lick at exactly the right moment is worth a dozen taps poorly timed and placed," he said. "She'll learn."

They started up the road, the filly walking between them. Alec put a hand on her neck, rubbing it gently. She had a mind of her own, but she'd come around, all right.

After she had worked off some of her excess energy by running around the paddock, he would ride her for the first time. He wouldn't have any trouble. He could stick with any kind of a rough colt, so he wasn't worrying about that. And the moment he sat in the saddle he would know a lot more about her than he did now—perhaps even more than Henry. He wanted to be pleased and happy with what he found. He wanted Black Minx to be the filly Henry thought she was.

Before Henry turned the filly loose in the paddock, he had Alec go up to the far end to flag her down if she built up too much speed. Leaning against the fence, Alec waited. He saw her go over to look at Napoleon in the next paddock. The old gelding pricked his ears, then drew back, a little startled, as Black Minx bolted up the field, kicking out her hind legs.

Alec watched her closely as she neared him and then cut across the paddock. She had gone smoothly into her gallop, so much like the Black and so unlike Satan, whose first movements were heavy and ponderous. Alec liked what he saw, and his gaze shifted to Henry at the other end of the paddock. He knew Henry was enjoying the filly's action, too.

Black Minx stopped suddenly to rear high and paw the air. When she came down, she was off again with lightning swiftness. Alec knew then she'd never be left at the post, not with such getaway speed. But would she be able to maintain her speed over a distance? Some horses were built for sprints, some for distances. Her smallness made him think she might be a speed horse, a sprinter. But Henry maintained she would be able to go a classic distance, the full mile and a quarter at which the Kentucky Derby was run. *Well, why shouldn't she be able to go the distance?* Alec asked himself. *Wasn't her sire the greatest distance runner of them all?*

Again the filly came up to Alec's end of the paddock. But this time she brought herself to an abrupt stop a short way from him. She reared, pawing the air, and whinnied shrilly. She even took a few steps on her hind legs, walking with the perfect balance and grace of a ballet dancer.

Alec didn't move. It was a pretty trick to see, but just now it had no place in her training as a racehorse.

"None of that, girl," he called to Black Minx.

Finally she came down and stood still, as though waiting for him to make a move, to run, so she could chase him. But he remained still and, after a few minutes, she snorted and bolted away. After going a short distance, she stopped, whirled, and came back to stand before him again. Her eyes were bright in her eagerness to play.

Alec watched the filly closely, knowing that she was more apt to try her tricks with him than with Henry. He was more the age and size of the Chandler kids, who had played with her so long. But he would have none of it. He would do nothing to hinder Henry's work in making her the racehorse he wanted her to be.

Black Minx's large eyes never left Alec. She moved a step nearer to extend her head toward him, her muzzle quivering excitedly. Alec waited, talking to her in a low voice but never moving. His hands remained at his sides. He did nothing to encourage her to come closer, to search his pockets, to nip, to play.

Suddenly she snorted again, tossing her head up and down with mane and forelock flying. Alec still didn't move, and finally she turned away from him, holding her head and docked tail high. Her manner was one of disdain and disappointment.

Her name suited her well, for certainly she was a little minx, Alec decided. Minx meant a pert girl, one inclined to be forward, impudent, even intentionally mischievous. Well, that was this filly all over!

He saw Henry move toward her as she stood by the fence, watching Napoleon. Apparently the old trainer thought it was time to take control again. She had stretched her legs and worked off the edge of her abundant energy. Alec knew that Henry hadn't enjoyed watching her tricks, her playfulness. From now on she wouldn't get a chance to frolic alone. From now on she would leave the barn only under saddle.

Alec waited until Henry had skillfully maneuvered the filly into the corner of the paddock. When the trainer had her by the halter, Alec started down.

More than ever he was anxious to ride her. He had liked her easy way of going about the paddock. But only when they had her on the track would they be able to learn what kind of racehorse she would be. Her mischief and bad manners could be corrected. More important were her speed over a distance, a will to win, and gameness. All three were necessary if she was to become a champion. Within a few minutes they'd start up the long road that would give them their answers during the months to come.

Henry was waving to Alec, urging him to quicken his steps. He broke into a trot, but continued thinking of the filly.

She had a mind of her own, and that to him indicated she'd inherited some of the Black's temperament. Not all of it, thank heavens. No more than Satan had. A little of it went a long way. Then certainly she should have *his* tremendous will to win and gameness! Alec's eyes were shining brightly as he neared Henry and Black Minx.

"Get the tack now," Henry said.

Alec nodded and went on to the tack room in the stallion barn. A few moments later he helped Henry put on the filly's bridle. She gave them no trouble with it or with the light saddle that they placed snugly on her back. She had worn each in her stall the week before, and was used to them again.

Henry clasped his hands, ready for Alec's knee. His face was serious, even a little grim. "I don't know how long it's been since she's had anyone on her back," he said quietly.

Alec raised his leg and was boosted up. He knew Henry wasn't worrying about his ability to stay on the filly. The trainer's concern was mostly due to wondering how she'd look to him under saddle. Henry, too, was well aware that this was the beginning of the road which would take Black Minx to the Derby post or end in her complete failure as a racehorse. Alec felt the light black body beneath him quiver, then shift uneasily.

Henry held her by the bridle. "Stick with her," he said, "but don't force her unless you have to. Go slow so you can feel her out."

Alec nodded, taking up rein as Henry left to close the paddock gate. The filly slid quickly to the side but Alec moved just as fast. He felt out her mouth and pressed his knees a little tighter against her sliding body. He talked to her all the while. Finally she came to a stop.

Henry returned to take hold again of her bridle. He led her past the stallion barn, and the filly's only sudden move was to turn her head toward Napoleon, who stood at his paddock gate watching them.

After going a short distance, Alec said, "Let me have her, Henry. If she's going to try anything, I'd rather have her do it here in the field than on the track."

Henry's hand left the bridle. "Okay, Alec. Jog her over, then give her a gallop of a mile and a quarter. A slow gallop unless I give you the word to step it up a bit. That's all I want today."

Henry dropped behind them. For a moment the filly

stayed at her fast walk, then her ears came back. Alec smiled. It was as if she had just realized she was alone with him and free of Henry for the first time. Tossing her black head, she moved into a jog. Alec rose in his short stirrups, talking to her all the while.

And now he realized more than ever that she wasn't as small as she looked. Her parts were so well put together that she just seemed small until you rode her.

"Act nicely now," he said softly. "Easy now, girl."

Black Minx's heavy mane was tossed back against Alec's head. He felt her mouth working on the bit. She was feeling him out just as he was doing with her. She turned her ears at the sound of his voice. Quickly, jerkily, she moved them back and forth. He believed she was trying to decide just how far she could go with him. Suddenly she tried to find out. She swerved abruptly, seeking to unseat him. But he moved with her, his knees and hands firm. Finally he straightened her out again.

"You can't get away with it," he told her softly.

The filly grabbed the bit and bolted. Alec's hands gave in to her, but only for a second. Then they moved quickly and he had the bit loose from between her clenched teeth. He brought her down to the jog Henry had ordered.

"I told you not to try it." He patted her neck.

She extended her head, wanting more rein. She stayed quiet, so he gave in a little. Again he felt her teeth champing on the bit, still feeling him out, not yet ready to admit that he was able to outguess her. He was ready when she swerved once more. His hands and knees tightened as he went with her, then straightened her out again.

For the remaining distance to the track the filly gave him

no trouble. Alec rubbed her neck fondly. She knew just how far she could go with him. Perhaps she'd be a good little girl from now on.

He jogged her halfway up the track, then turned, awaiting Henry's signal to gallop. He was to take her a mile and a quarter, two and a half times around their half-mile training track. He turned to the field beyond but couldn't see the Black. The stallion was down in the ravine. Henry waved his hand, and Alec gave the filly some rein.

She moved quickly into her gallop, and the smoothness of her gait caused Alec to think again of how like her sire she was. He pressed his head close to her neck. "Come on, you little Black," he said excitedly. "Come on!"

Like her great sire, she kept her head high and her ears pricked forward while she galloped. Alec felt the flowing power, controlled now, but promising a world of speed when he asked for it.

They passed Henry, and Alec wanted to shout to him that here was a fine filly. Here was one with extreme speed, a filly worthy of her great heritage. But he controlled his enthusiasm. He would give her more rein. Let Henry see a little of it for himself.

His hands moved forward as he took her into the first turn. "Now, Minx," he said. "I'll let you go a little more." He began clucking in her ear.

She moved close to the rail, her strides never faltering. But neither did they pick up any speed. A shadow of concern passed over Alec's face. They came off the turn and entered the backstretch. She may have been a little afraid of the turn, Alec decided. He gave her more rein, clucking to her again. "Now, girl! Let's pick them up."

Her strides neither lengthened nor came faster. Still moving smoothly, she made no effort to increase her gallop in spite of the slack rein, the clucking in her ear. Alec slid closer to her neck, talking to her, urging her on. But her only response was the constant flicking of her small ears, forward and back. All through the backstretch, around the turn, and down the homestretch she continued her slow, easy gallop.

Henry shouted, when they passed, "That's good, Alec, but move her up a little on the next round!"

*Move her up a little!* Alec grimaced at Henry's instructions. He sat quietly in the saddle, feeling miserable for Henry, for himself. He couldn't get an ounce more speed out of this filly. She knew what she was doing, and what he wanted from her. But she just wouldn't run for him! Perhaps a whip would bring the speed out of her. But forcing a horse to race with a stick wasn't for him or Henry or Hopeful Farm.

Alec took the filly into the first turn again, sick with disappointment in this first daughter of the Black.

*Sires are only half,* he reminded himself.

*But this filly is out of a good mare. And she has the Black's looks and temperament. She has the Black's speed!* He could feel it in her every movement. Yet she wouldn't use it, and neither he nor Henry would ever beat it out of her with a whip.

The reins were slack against her neck. He kept talking to her, urging her, as they once more entered the backstretch. But she did not respond. Suddenly Alec heard the Black's shrill whistle. The filly bolted, her strides finally coming faster.

Alec caught a glimpse of the stallion moving over the hilltop in his field. Then the Black was plunging toward the high, wooden-barred fence which ran parallel with the track for the length of the backstretch.

His sudden appearance had frightened the filly, for she galloped hard. She bore down upon the back turn. She ran low, her strides coming long and fast. Alec pressed his head hard against her neck and let her go.

Coming off the turn, she slowed as suddenly as her terrified flight had begun. She settled back into her easy gallop, turning her head to look across the track's infield where the Black raced up and down the fence.

Alec took her past Henry again, then into the turn for the last quarter of a mile which had been ordered. As they neared the Black, she watched him but she was no longer frightened. She didn't break stride even when the stallion settled down to run along the pasture fence beside her.

Finishing the full distance, Alec drew back on the reins. She fought him furiously, but he got her down to a jog. "You're a contrary filly," he said bitterly. "I don't know what Henry's going to do with you."

When he took her the rest of the way around the track, he was afraid to look at Henry. He was certain that his eyes would tell the story of his disappointment in the filly.

Taking Black Minx's bridle, Henry said severely, "I didn't tell you to breeze her, Alec. You took her too fast that one furlong. She's not ready for it." Then he added more softly, "But I guess it didn't hurt her any."

"She made that fast move only because the Black frightened her," Alec said. "I didn't have anything to do with it. She loafed all the rest of the time. I couldn't even make her gallop faster as you wanted me to do."

For a moment Henry's face sobered, then lightened. "She's

got the speed in her. I'll find a way to get it out when we're ready for her breezes and fast works." He raised a hand to stroke Black Minx's head. When she tried to nip him he had no alternative but to slap her on the muzzle. "I guess I got a Derby horse, all right, Alec. I guess I have."

Alec sat back in the saddle. At the moment he didn't think Black Minx ever would be ready to race, much less start in the Kentucky Derby. But all that was best unsaid.

# Hot Potato

## 5

The month of December brought no change in Henry's optimistic belief that he would have Black Minx all set to race by the following spring. He discussed with Alec's father, who had charge of the farm and racing stable budgets, the nomination payments which would be due the middle of February. These sums of money had to be paid in order to make the filly eligible for the Kentucky Oaks at a mile and a sixteenth, and, more important, for the Kentucky Derby at a mile and a quarter. Both races were to be held at Churchill Downs, Louisville, Kentucky, during the first week in May.

Henry told Alec that although Black Minx was owned by him he wanted her to race in the black-and-white colors of Hopeful Farm. He also insisted that any money she won would be invested in their farm operation and in the training of their horses.

Alec saw no reason for Henry's high hopes of racing Black Minx successfully. He continued riding her daily, galloping from a mile and a quarter to sometimes two or three miles, according to Henry's instructions, and never once did she make the slightest attempt to move faster. Henry didn't offer to explain why he thought he could overcome the filly's loafing, nor did he tell what he was going to do to accomplish this feat. And Alec did not ask him. He rode Black Minx only as he was ordered, and let it go at that.

She was easier under saddle now, seldom making any attempt to unseat him. She had learned that his reflexes were as fast as her own, that he was alert and ready for her every move. But she wouldn't run for him, and there was nothing he could do about it without resorting to a whip, the use of which neither he nor Henry approved.

"Besides, it still wouldn't get any speed out of her," Henry told him one day. "Use a whip on her and she'd take you through the rail, same as she did Nino Nella in Florida last year."

"She was a two-year-old then. Don't they have a rule at Hialeah Park that jockeys can't carry or use whips in two-year-old races?" Alec had asked.

"Sure. But Nella used his hand, spanking her, when she didn't move for him. That's against the rule, too. He was fined by the judges."

"Getting a fine on top of a broken collarbone couldn't have made him very happy with this filly."

"No, I wouldn't think so. Nella's out in California now. He sure wasn't right for Black Minx. He's a 'huffle-scuffle' rider, using his hands and feet every second to get the most out of his mounts. This filly has too much of the Black in her for that kind of riding. Try to force the speed out of her with hands or feet and she'll balk good. I guess we understand that, all right."

Alec understood, but it didn't help any in riding her on her daily workouts. She had become part of his day, and his days were full, although Henry continued to help with the farm chores. Fortunately the weather, for the most part, remained good and they were able to turn out the horses every day.

In the early afternoon of the first Saturday in January, Alec left the stallion barn. A cold rain was falling and he knew he wouldn't be riding Black Minx. Nevertheless he made his way toward her barn. The next hour belonged to the filly, and Alec seldom veered from his schedule.

The freezing rain pelted his face, so he pulled the hood of his jacket over his cap and hunched his shoulders. Henry wouldn't be in a happy mood with this kind of weather. Still, there had been few days like it, many less than Henry had dared hope for. Alec wondered if any candidate for the Kentucky Derby had ever been trained so far north. Most of this season's top three-year-olds were wintering in Florida, California, and the Carolinas. But the weather here had been good to them so far. He hoped it would continue to be.

Even so, could he believe that Black Minx would one day be ready for the Derby? Sliding open the barn door, he went inside, angrily casting off his misgivings. *If Henry said she would be ready, she would be.* Henry knew what he was doing.

Going to the filly's stall, he found Henry grooming her. She tried to turn her head at his approach but the short rope held her too close. She whinnied, pawing at the straw until she found the clay floor beneath.

Henry stopped her pawing, then turned to Alec. "Awful day," he said.

"Awful."

"Too bad," Henry said, running his cloth down the filly's legs. "She needed the work."

Alec stepped inside the stall. Black Minx turned her head toward him. He saw the restlessness in her eyes. She wanted to get out. "Not today," he told her.

She tossed her head but stood surprisingly still beneath Henry's hand. Once more Alec marveled at the change Henry had brought about in her stable manners. Very seldom did she rear or paw. Her only fault was nipping. She was still inclined to do that in spite of Henry's careful and patient handling.

Henry swept the cloth over the filly's level back. Alec noticed how fine she looked. The long and frequent gallops had done her a world of good. Her body glistened with supple muscle, in all the right places. That she could look so much like the Black, that she could possess so much of his speed and still not want to run, were the reasons for Alec's great disappointment in her. Courage and the will to respond and win a race were the qualities he most respected in her great sire. The Black had given these to Satan, but not to this filly. *Why?*

Alec heard himself say, "It's such a pity." He stopped suddenly in a futile effort to choke back his words, to keep them from Henry.

The trainer turned. "A pity, Alec?" He studied the boy's face. "You mean y'still don't think I'm going to get her to run the way I know she can?"

Alec shook his head. "I know you can do it, Henry." He tried to sound sincere.

Henry smiled. "Sure I can, Alec. I'll get the best out of her the wisest way. I know the key that'll turn it all loose. You'll see." He became excited, his eyes shining brightly. "This is just what makes the handling of a colt or filly by the Black the most exciting thing in the world, Alec. You don't train 'em by the book. No, you think and probe, and feel your way along to find the right key that sets the works off. Then you have a real racehorse!"

"You're right. I know—" Alec stopped suddenly, his gaze shifting to the filly. Henry had moved closer to her head during their conversation, and now she was reaching for his arm, her teeth bared. "Watch out, Henry!"

His warning came too late. The filly bit Henry high on his left arm. Then she drew back, tossing her head. Henry's lips were clenched tight in pain and his right hand gripped the injured arm.

Outside the stall Alec reached for the torn sweater but Henry brushed his hand aside. "It's all right," he said.

"You'd better get to a doctor."

"Why? I've been bitten before and I'm still around."

"It's bleeding," Alec said.

"I know it is. I'll treat it myself."

"I still think you should see a doctor," Alec repeated, although he knew his advice wouldn't be taken. "She wasn't playing this time," he added.

"No." Henry turned away from the filly and from Alec too. He started down the barn.

Alec caught up with him at the foot of the stairs that led to Henry's apartment. "What are you going to do?"

"Fix my arm *first*." Henry's footsteps were hard on the stairs.

"And then?" Alec asked anxiously.

Henry was in his bathroom before he answered, "I'm going to tighten the grip on her. I tried being nice but it didn't do much good. Now she's got to learn once and for all. If I let her go, she'll be taking my hand off one of these days. Even if she's playin' I won't like it none."

He removed his torn sweater and shirt, disclosing the two clean cuts from the filly's upper and lower teeth. The wound was still bleeding. "Get me that bottle of antiseptic in the medicine chest there," he said. "And the cotton and gauze."

"You'd better let me do it," Alec said impatiently. "There are some things you can't do all by yourself, especially with only one hand."

"I can use both hands," Henry said, moving his injured arm.

"Keep it still. You're making it bleed all the more." Alec poured the antiseptic on a swab of cotton and cleaned the wound. The bleeding was beginning to stop. "You won't see a doctor. You've got a mind of your own just like the filly. You're a good pair."

"Now the bandage," Henry said, ignoring Alec's criticism.

When the bandage was on, Henry again moved his arm in spite of Alec's protests. He put on a clean shirt and another sweater, then went to the kitchen.

Alec heard the sharp clang of a cooking pot against the stove. He arrived in the kitchen to see Henry drop a large potato in the pot. "What are you doing?"

"Boiling myself a potato." And with that Henry sat down in a chair, offering nothing more by way of explanation.

Alec sat down, too. He waited until the steam began to raise the lid of the pot. Then he said, "You're not going to eat that potato?"

"No."

"Then what are you going to do with it?" Alec's forehead became wrinkled with concern.

"It's a little trick I use only when I have to," Henry said finally.

"Maybe you ought to wait until tomorrow, Henry. Maybe you're sore at her now. You might do something you wouldn't ordinarily do."

Henry smiled. "I'm not sore at her, Alec. I got too close without paying attention to her. It's just that I've got to stop her now or she might do *real* injury to one of us next time."

"Will it hurt her?"

"She won't like it," Henry said. "But she won't forget it, either. It's worked before; it'll work now. I've tried bein' nice, and it didn't pay off."

Alec asked no further questions.

Henry went to the closet just off the kitchen and began rummaging around the upper shelf. Alec knew he kept a lot of patent bits and gadgets there which they very seldom had any occasion to use. Finally Henry returned, carrying only a slender, round stick about two feet long; it narrowed to a sharp point at one end. It was this end which he thrust into the potato. Then he carried it to the sink and ran cold water over the potato just long enough to kill the steamy odor.

"Henry, you're not going to stick that in her mouth!"

"No, I won't make the move. She'll be the one to do it—that is, if she tries to bite me again."

Henry went to the closet once more, this time to get a sponge which he placed carefully beneath his sweater near the shoulder of his good arm. Then he returned to Alec. "Slide the stick down the sleeve now," he said. "Keep the potato against the sponge there. I don't want it touching my shirt. It's hot."

"I know it."

When Alec had finished, the trainer buttoned his sweater again and, taking a heavy rubber band, ran it around his wrist to keep the stick steady and the potato in position.

By this time Alec knew what Henry was going to do. He would groom the filly, getting close enough to her head so that she could bite him if she wanted to. But this time instead of tearing Henry's flesh, she would sink her teeth into the boiled potato, burning her mouth.

"She might hate you forever for it," Alec said. "This trick might undo all the good your gentling has done for her."

"No," Henry said, "the secret to the success of this trick is that I have the freedom of my hands. I'll just be standing there grooming her as I always do. She won't connect my hands with anything that happens to her. She'll know only that when she bit me she hurt herself. And I have yet to see a horse that forgets this lesson and wants to bite anyone again." He paused. "I don't like to burn her. But in a way it's a lot like a parent letting his child put a finger on a stove to teach him that it's hot and to prevent a more serious injury later on. Well, maybe I'm doing just about the same thing here. She'll burn her mouth. But it won't be anything serious, and she'll have learned her lesson."

"*If* she bites," Alec said.

"Yeah, that's right. She may not. I don't know."

"And," Alec said, "if she does, you'd better make certain her teeth hit the potato and not your arm again. If she does, you *will* have to go to the doctor."

"Don't worry. I'll make certain of that."

They went to Black Minx.

"Stay outside the stall," Henry said, picking up his soft brush.

Alec watched him walk up to the filly and talk to her softly. She pricked her ears at his reappearance and watched him out of the corners of her large eyes. Henry stayed away from her head, running the brush over her back and humming to her. His right arm, with the concealed stick and potato, was straight and rigid.

For a long while Henry continued grooming her back and hindquarters, seemingly in no hurry to approach her head. She stopped watching him and her head ceased its tossing. She was enjoying the soft touch of the brush, and Henry was giving her every chance to behave like a well-mannered filly. But finally he began moving toward her neck. He brushed her mane for a while. Her head remained still. Henry went a little more to the front of her, running the brush down her long neck. His right shoulder was close to the filly's head. Now she was watching him. She tossed her head.

Alec knew she'd be able to reach Henry now if she tried. But Black Minx made no move, and Henry continued his grooming and humming. Nevertheless Alec saw that the old trainer was ready for her. As the minutes ticked away, it looked as though there would be no need for any lesson.

Then Alec noticed the sudden trembling of the filly's black body. A moment later she shifted her feet restlessly and began tossing her head angrily. It was as if she suddenly had decided that she'd been well-mannered long enough and the time had come to reestablish her independence. Her stump of a tail moved back and forth like a car's windshield wiper. She continued tossing her head. She was not getting her own way and she didn't like it. Henry kept brushing her neck, his right shoulder close to her mouth. Suddenly her ears swept back. She nipped at him but missed. Henry paid no attention to her; he kept at his grooming.

Alec did not believe the filly had intended to reach Henry that time. Perhaps her bold, precocious mind had meant it only as a warning to Henry that she wanted her own way.

The sound of the filly's hoofs moving in the straw and Henry's humming went on for a few more minutes. Then the hoof movements stopped. Black Minx reached for Henry and there was no stopping this time. She bit his bulging arm!

Her head came back fast, her eyes showing how startled she was. Henry never stopped his grooming to look at her. But Alec was watching. She had bitten squarely into the boiled potato. Her lips were drawn back and her mouth was working frantically. She kept it open and her incessant blowing filled the stall. Alec couldn't help smiling at her surprise and bewilderment.

All the while Henry continued working. He brushed her mane again, ran a cloth down her forelegs, even stooped beneath her head to clean her chest. But Black Minx's only movements were to work her mouth. She paid not the slightest attention to him.

Finally Henry left the stall and went with Alec to the far end of the barn. There he withdrew the stick from beneath his sweater, and they looked at the deep marks made in the potato by the filly's teeth. The escaping steam turned gray in the cool air of the barn.

"She hit it square," Henry said. "I'm going to stay around to make sure she's all right."

Alec said, "I hope it works."

"It will. I don't expect any more trouble from her."

"Even on the track?" Alec couldn't help asking. "You can't use a hot potato to cure her loafing, Henry."

The trainer smiled. "No, but I can outsmart her another way."

"Are you going to tell me just how you'll do it?"

"I'd rather show you," Henry said.

"When?"

"Are you pinning me down?" Henry asked.

"Sure."

"All right then," Henry said, still smiling. "We'll make it next Saturday, if the weather is good enough for us to get out on the track."

"You're really trying to be mysterious about it, aren't you, Henry?"

"Yep, I guess I am." Without another word the old trainer went back to the filly's stall.

Alec left the barn, wondering what other trick Henry had up his sleeve for Black Minx. He'd find out next Saturday.

# *Runaway!*

# 6

During that week, the weather became more what was to be expected for the middle of January in New York State. It turned very cold, verging near zero several nights. The ground froze.

Henry sent Black Minx to the track every day; only a cold rain or an icy track could force him to keep her in the barn. Her burned mouth ceased bothering her, and she no longer drew back her lips, baring her teeth to Henry or Alec. She seemed cured of nipping, just as Henry had said she would be.

Often, as Alec galloped her on these cold days, he couldn't help thinking that Henry might get this black filly to the Kentucky Derby after all. If one trick had proved successful, another might work, too. He never mentioned the coming Saturday to Henry, and his friend didn't bring it up either. From all that went on between them that week it was as if their conversation in the barn never had been.

Late Friday afternoon the snow began to fall. It continued through the night, and when it stopped on Saturday morning there were three good inches of it on the ground. Alec turned out all the horses, for he knew that snow was good for their legs and feet. He watched them at play in the paddocks and fields beneath an overcast sky, their winter coats somber with no sun to pick up the highlights. When he left the Black in the far field, he walked along the track, scuffing the snow. He didn't know if Henry would postpone whatever it was he had planned today for the filly. That is, if Henry still remembered his promise of a week ago.

Alec stooped to pick up a handful of snow. It was light and dry. His foot pushed the snow from the track until he came to the sandy loam beneath. It was hard, of course, just as it had been all week long. In fact, the track was in better shape than before for a fast work, for the snow provided a soft cushion.

Alec began walking again. He had a lot of work to do—stalls to clean, bedding down, grooming, and handling the three colts who had become yearlings as of the first of January. Even so, he eagerly looked forward to what might come when he rode Black Minx onto the track within a few hours.

It was a little after noon when Henry boosted him up on the filly. Except for the snow and Black Minx's liking for it, this moment was no different from the beginning of any other day's workout. Alec sat astride Black Minx outside the barn, awaiting any special instructions from Henry. None came.

The snow rose to the filly's fetlocks. She loved it. She kept moving her feet. Finally Henry led her up the road, past the stallion barn and paddocks, before turning her over completely to Alec. She made one of her rare moves to unseat him but he moved as one with her. The pressure of bit and knees brought her back in line again.

Henry said, "She knows you're always one step ahead of her, Alec."

The filly pranced to one side, flaying the snow. Her breath made two billowing streams of gray in the cold, crisp air. She felt good. She wanted to gallop. But Alec doubted that she'd move any faster for him on the track just because she felt so good.

He took her across the field, holding her to a jog so as to be within hearing distance of Henry's voice. Would today's instructions be the same as on all other days? Would Henry say, "Gallop her a mile . . . a mile and a half . . . two miles" and let it go at that, forgetting completely that this was *the day*?

Alec rose high in his stirrups, his head alongside her neck. The wind was cold. When she galloped it would become colder. If she really let out, it would be a bitter wind. But he'd welcome it. He might not even feel it. He'd be too excited if such a thing happened. Wait a minute now! He was getting ahead of himself. The chances were good that Henry had forgotten their talk. Henry was fine at that, especially when he thought it wiser not to remember.

Black Minx moved onto the track, or at least where it would have been if the snow hadn't covered it. Alec took her over near the rail so she'd know they had arrived. He talked to her while he let her move into her lope going up the track. Then he brought her to a stop, turned, and waited for

Henry. He pulled down his peaked cap hard upon his head and over his ears. He buttoned the top of his jacket and turned up his collar. Come what might, he was ready.

Standing in the same spot, the filly moved her feet in the snow, still playing. Alec watched Henry coming up the track. He was in a half-run to keep warm, his bowlegs spinning like a wheel. Henry's face indicated nothing exceptional to come; as always before a session on the track, it was sober and serious.

"What'll it be, Henry?"

The trainer stood at the saddle now. When he gave his instructions, his words were the same as those of the day before and the day before that. "Gallop her a mile, Alec. That'll be enough."

Alec turned his eyes away. That was that. He'd wasted his time even thinking, wondering about it. He moved forward in his saddle, ready to go.

"Wait a minute, Alec."

He sat back once more. "Yes, Henry?"

"We're going to work her a fast quarter today. Not that she needs it yet, but because of what we talked about last week. It won't hurt her none. She's good and hard from galloping."

Alec's eyes were wide. It had come. "How do I get this *fast* quarter out of her?"

Henry's words were terse, clipped, all business. "Take her the usual gallop for three-quarters. I don't care if you try to urge her to go faster or not. It doesn't matter to me, so suit yourself. But when you hit the last quarter pole I want you to do a simple thing. I want you to let her take hold of the bit, and don't take it away from her like I know you can do.

But I want you to try. Give her the idea you've lost control, that she's running away with you, that you can't get the bit from her. That's all I want you to do, Alec. We'll see what happens." Henry stepped back. "Go ahead now."

Alec didn't remember sending off the filly. Henry's words still rang in his ears. He thought about them all down the stretch and into the first turn. He didn't feel the cold wind on his face. He let the filly gallop as she pleased.

So simple, if it worked! And why shouldn't it work? He had known all along that she had a mind of her own, that she was a contrary little filly. How often had he said that she was most likely to do just the opposite of what he wanted? Many times! Yet it had taken Henry to figure out that her headstrong temperament might be used to their advantage. Henry had said he was going to outsmart her. Well, if this trick worked, he'd be doing just that!

They were in the backstretch when Alec began clucking to her. He'd better urge her to go faster as he had always done. She might think it strange if he didn't, and he wanted everything to be the same until that last quarter. He could hardly wait. He was tense, excited. He decided he'd better relax or she'd sense the difference in him. She was that smart.

She went down the backstretch, moving lightly over the snow and enjoying every stride she took. Her ears flicked back at his words, her mane waving beside him. He felt her mouth on the bit, toying and playing with it even as she galloped. Whenever she'd grabbed the bit in the past he'd taken it away without much trouble. But soon it would be different. Soon he'd let her take the bit. He'd led her hold on to it. *Run away with him!* So simple, so easy. Would it work?

They swept past Henry, entering the last half-mile. Alec

tried to move her faster, urging and coaxing. But her strides kept coming the same distance apart, no longer, no faster. Alec felt her powerful hindquarters carrying him along almost effortlessly. He became excited again at the potential speed she had to give.

Around the first turn once more, then they were at the top of the backstretch. The last quarter-mile would begin halfway down the track. Alec got ready.

Hunched forward, he concentrated on the working of her mouth. He forgot everything else. He moved his hands, carefully, gently. He felt her moving the bit, ready to grab it. He let her alone this time. She played with the bit some more, then suddenly had it between her teeth!

Alec's hands moved quickly. But not too fast, not too hard. He didn't want to be successful in getting the bit away from her. Not now! Instead he began calling, "Whoa!" in her ear. He started sawing the reins lightly against the corners of her mouth, but never hard enough to dislodge the bit from between her clenched teeth.

The quarter pole flashed by and Black Minx was in full flight! Alec felt the release of her hard muscles beneath him and the tremendous quickening of her strides. He saw the rail posts go by with ever-increasing speed. But he paid little attention to all this as he concentrated on making the filly think he'd lost control of her.

No longer did he cluck in her ear, urging her to gallop faster. Instead his words were a constant stream of *whoa*'s which served only to drive her on to greater speed. The wind cut his face. He wanted to smile but couldn't. He worked his hands against her mouth, but this, too, only made her go faster.

She was running away with him! And she ran the way any-one in the world would love to see his horse run. Her strides swept over the snow with the speed of the wind. She held her head high but pushed hard against the bit. She never moved it in her breathtaking flight beneath the gray, flat winter sky. She rounded the back turn with no lurching or swaying of head or body. Her every stride was the ultimate in grace and beauty, in balance and speed.

As they came down the homestretch and neared Henry, Alec's frantic calls of "Whoa!" rang above the pounding of her hoofs in the snow. He let her go until they had left Henry behind and had passed the finish line. Then he stopped sawing her mouth. He gave her loose rein and felt her grip on the bit relax a little. He pulled back in sudden movement. Again he gave loose rein, then drew back, saw-ing. This time he worked the bit free. She tossed her head, fighting him for many strides before she realized that he was in full control once more. Only then did she slow down.

He turned her and started back toward Henry. Black Minx pranced and snorted constantly as if to let Alec know she had had her way for a short while anyway. He smiled and patted her sweaty neck. It was good that she seemed to feel this way.

Henry hurried up to them. "Keep her moving, Alec," he said. "I don't want her to catch cold."

"Couldn't keep her still if I tried."

Henry took hold of the filly's bridle and started off for the barns at a fast walk. "We'll rub her down real good," he said.

"She did it, all right," Alec said.

"Sure. I told you we had a Derby horse. Like I said, you just can't train this filly by the book. She'll run for us any time we let her think she's got full control of the situation. It's as simple as that."

"It's simple now that you've thought of it," Alec said. He pushed the heavy black mane away to pat her neck. Her head was set beautifully, almost delicately, on her long, high-crested neck. She looked like the Black and there was no doubt now that she had inherited his speed. Henry had found a way to get it out of her. Still, it was a great pity that she had to be tricked into running and didn't have the will to race and win as did her sire. Speed alone wasn't enough to make her a champion. Or was it, since she possessed so much of it? Only in the Kentucky Derby would they learn the answer.

# *The Yardstick*

## 7

Black Minx wasn't given a fast work again. For the rest of January and into February, Alec continued galloping her almost every day. Henry was happy that the weather remained cold and dry, despite occasional snow, and that he was able to get his filly onto the track to gallop and develop in body and wind. She was hard and never blew after her long sessions on the track.

Not once did Alec use the key Henry had given him to get more speed from Black Minx. Her training was in Henry's hands, and speed wasn't ordered. Alec knew it would be March before her fast works would begin in preparation for the spring races.

During February his responsibility at the farm became heavier. Outside mares began arriving, to be bred to the Black and Satan. He relinquished many of his chores to the three hired men from the nearby village, who had assisted him the year before during the foaling and breeding season. But he assumed other duties. He did more paper work, more field work, in order to learn everything possible about each mare's breeding history before mating her to his stallions.

Except for an hour each day he seldom saw Black Minx. Yet the filly was always entering his thoughts even though he tried to keep her out of them because of his other work.

Tonight was a good example. It was ten o'clock and Alec sat behind the huge desk in the stallion barn office. He still had a good hour's work left on the breeding chart before him. His father had taken all bookings of outside mares to the Black and Satan. Eight mares had already arrived at the farm, and there were sixteen more to come. Seventeen mares were in foal. Five of them would foal later this month, six during March, three during April, and three in May.

Alec began listing the mares' names and their breeding records on the chart, which from now until late May would be his daily bible.

While writing, he caught himself thinking of Black Minx from time to time. For a long while he successfully pushed her out of his mind. Finally he relaxed in his chair to think only of her. He didn't like the black filly to interfere with his farm work. Yet if he had something on his mind it was far better to face it than to allow his thoughts to stray while he was trying to concentrate on the field chart.

*Well, what is it this time?* he asked himself. *Haven't I decided that her training and racing are Henry's jobs? Haven't I decided to let well enough alone and to be content with just managing the farm? Henry's the head of the racing stable. He has all the answers. He's satisfied with her. Why shouldn't I be?*

*But how will Henry ever get anyone to ride her shrewdly in a race? A jockey has only split seconds in which to make decisions. His mount must respond when asked to try for an opening or to wait. Black Minx won't go along with such practices. She'll run only when she thinks she has full control. Therefore, what good will it do for her jockey to be a good judge of pace, to know when to make his bid and when to lay back? The filly will have none of that. She'll run herself out, for what horse can go the limit of his speed from starting post to finish?*

Alec thought about this problem for a long while before going back to work on his chart. He arrived at no answer. He didn't think there was any. But having had it out with himself made it easier to concentrate on his work. Besides, it was Henry's problem.

Later, when he left the stallion barn, it was snowing again. He zipped up his jacket as he walked toward the house. After going a short way he stopped to look at the startling white-ness of the paddocks and fields, all so beautiful in the falling snow. He turned to the darkened house. He didn't feel like going to bed right away. Just then he noticed the light in Henry's apartment, and started for it.

Climbing the stairs, he heard low music coming from Henry's radio. He knocked on the door, and then went in-side. "Busy?" he asked.

Without leaving his chair, Henry turned off the radio and put down the magazine he had been reading. "Well, believe it or not, I've been working."

Alec sat down next to him. "Reading horse magazines is a swell way of making a living," he said.

"Sure. What have you been doing?"

"Working on my field chart."

"I've been working on a chart too," Henry said, tossing the magazine into Alec's lap.

Alec looked down at the page opened before him. The heading read, "Names and Weights for the Experimental Free Handicaps." What followed was a rating of that year's three-year-olds. It took into consideration their racing records of the year before, when they had been two-year-olds, and their prospects for racing over the longer distances as three-year-olds. There were one hundred and five horses listed, and each was assigned the weight he must carry if he were to go to the post for the running of the Experimental Free Handicaps held in April. This list was worth studying, for the track handicapper who made it had a reputation for forecasting accurately the top three-year-olds each year.

Alec turned to Henry. "I see he's got Silver Jet at the top of the list."

"Yeah, he figures that the colt will be able to go the distance and win some classics this year."

"He should," Alec said. "He's a good colt."

"Tom Flint thinks so, too," Henry said. "I saw him at the Kentucky sales. He thinks so much of his Silver Jet that he paid sixty-six thousand dollars for a full-brother yearling."

"Don't you like him?" Alec asked.

"Sure. Silver Jet is a fine colt, plenty fine. He should be right up front come Derby Day, if nothing happens to him before then."

Alec turned back to the magazine. He noticed Henry's penciled check marks alongside the names of a few horses. "Why the checks, Henry?" he asked without taking his eyes off the list.

Moving closer, Henry placed a heavy, square-tipped finger

on the page. "I figure," he said, "that of all these three-year-olds there are five who in my opinion stand the best chance of copping the Derby. The two at the top, Silver Jet and Eclipse, certainly should be strong contenders. Further down the list here I've marked one I like too. He's a California-bred colt named Golden Vanity. He wasn't raced heavily last year at two, but what he did was most impressive. To me, anyway," he added hastily.

His finger moved again. "And here's a Virginia colt called Wintertime, who was improving fast toward the end of last season. I think he'll continue moving up this year, and work his way right up with the others by Derby time."

Henry's finger dropped almost to the bottom of the list. "And the last I've marked is Lady Lee, who will bear watch—"

"A filly?" Alec interrupted.

"Yeah, and I think a good one. She likes distance and just might go a mile and a quarter."

Henry sat back in his chair, and Alec put down the magazine.

"Pretty soon now," Henry said, "we'll be able to tell a little more about these horses."

"You mean in the Santa Anita Derby?"

Henry nodded. "Golden Vanity will be in that race."

"When is it run?"

"February twenty-fourth. That's next Saturday."

Alec picked up the magazine again and thumbed its pages but he was not really looking for anything in particular. In the midst of all his farm work he seldom had a chance to remember that the Kentucky Derby was more than just one big race in May for any number of three-year-olds. Many of them even now were at the racetrack, ready to begin the long trek that might lead to the winner's circle of the Kentucky Derby.

From next Saturday until the first Saturday in May, there would be races such as the Santa Anita Derby, the Flamingo, the Experimental Handicaps, and the Wood Memorial—to name only a few. They were all important races in themselves, but they were also considered preparatory races to the greatest American classic of them all, the Kentucky Derby. Actually, some were good tests for Derby candidates and some weren't. Alec believed that the races to be run this month and next came much too early in the year to rank as truly significant tests. And not one of all these preparatory races was over the Derby distance of a full mile and a quarter. Yet they bore watching, for from these races usually emerged the Derby winner.

But not always. A few three-year-olds had arrived unheralded, even untried, at the Kentucky Derby post and had gone on to win. Might not Black Minx be one of these?

Alec looked up from the magazine. "I'd forgotten it was all starting so soon," he said. "I thought we could wait until May before getting excited about the big one."

Henry smiled. "Plenty of people are becoming excited right now, hoping their colts and fillies will show something in the prep races to prove themselves worthy of taking up space at the Derby post. But we don't need to get excited—not yet. We got lots of time."

"Then you think our filly is worthy of a post position without racing in any of the preps?"

"I think so, Alec. We'll just sit back for the time bein' and watch the show. It all starts next Saturday, and since the

Santa Anita race will be on television, all we have to do is watch what happens."

"And, meanwhile, continue galloping Black Minx," Alec said quietly.

"Oh, sure," Henry said. "Sure."

"Good night, Henry."

" 'Night, Alec."

# *The Santa Anita Derby*

## 8

On Saturday evening, the twenty-fourth of February, Alec and Henry sat before the television screen ready to watch the running of the Santa Anita Derby in California. They were in the small but comfortably furnished attic to which Mrs. Ramsay had relegated the television set after having had it in her living room for one week. She had decided that television certainly had a place in their new house, but she wasn't going to let it play havoc with her home life—her sewing, her reading, and her conversations with her family. Therefore it should have a room all its own, where they could go to watch any favorite program.

Henry slouched in a deep armchair. Impatiently he glanced at the variety show now on the screen; then he looked at his wrist watch. "They'd better get off soon," he grumbled.

Alec said, "Five minutes more. The telecast of the race isn't scheduled until then."

Henry grunted.

Alec turned to the window. Outside it had been dark for hours. But within minutes they'd be taken to California and it would be late afternoon on race day. He pulled his chair a little closer to the set. He didn't want to miss a thing.

Henry's eyes were now on the screen. The variety show ended, then came the station break. Another thirty seconds and they were at Santa Anita Park, Arcadia, California.

Twelve horses paraded to the post while the announcer welcomed his television audience to one of the top-ranking winter classics for three-year-olds, the Santa Anita Derby.

Heavy banks of clouds hung low over the track, but they did not detract from the beauty of the colts now moving gracefully past packed stands.

"Unfortunately, for the first day of this race meeting we have no sun," the announcer said. "It has been overcast all day long with no wind to blow the clouds away. However, the lack of our usual good weather has not kept many people from witnessing this great Winter Derby. We have a record crowd of sixty-eight thousand people here, some of whom arrived at six o'clock this morning to line up before the grandstand gates."

The picture left the horses to sweep over the throng that jammed the grandstand, the clubhouse, and the track's infield, where thousands were gathered along the rail.

"Get back to the horses, Mister," Henry growled.

The picture shifted to the post parade again as the announcer went on: "We have only one minute before post time. The race is a mile and an eighth in length, with a purse of eighty-nine thousand dollars waiting for the winner. Twelve three-year-olds are on their way to the post. All are colts, no fillies having been entered. The favorite is the California-bred colt Golden Vanity in number four post position. Naturally, the crowd here is eager to see him win. Sectional rivalry in this classic has always been keen and exciting, and today is no exception. Top eastern three-year-olds Moonstruck, High Up, Sadhu, and My Time are here and rated to give Golden Vanity a race all the way to the wire. But Californians sincerely believe they have another Morvich in Golden Vanity. Morvich, you know, was the only California-bred horse to win the Kentucky Derby, taking that classic in 1922. There are many here today who think Golden Vanity is the first horse foaled in California that is his equal."

The picture showed a close-up of Golden Vanity as he passed the starting gate and went up the track at a slow gallop, his jockey standing high in his stirrup irons.

It was easy for Alec and Henry to see why the colt had been given his name. He was a light chestnut and startlingly big for his age, about seventeen hands. His neck, body, and legs were long and so finely balanced that anyone would pause to look twice at him. His stride was long and elastic, and he moved with an air of arrogant pride. He tossed his handsome head continually and his body shifted nervously from one side to the other.

Watching him, Henry said, "He's beautiful but he looks overeager to me. He could use up most of his energy early in the race. If he does, the others will get to him at the end."

"We'll know in a minute," Alec said. "Isn't that Nino Nella up on him, Henry?"

"That's Nino Nella riding Golden Vanity," the announcer answered for Henry. "Don't let the colt's big size fool you into thinking Nino isn't just as small as he looks up there. This eighteen-year-old kid from Brooklyn, New York, weighs only eighty-two pounds. His riding has been sensational in this—his very first—season in California. Two years ago Nino was a plumber's helper in Brooklyn. Today he's the hottest jockey here at Santa Anita, with the most wins and money won during the season. They're saying around the track that horses like to run for Nino. And it certainly appears so. He's ridden Golden Vanity to his previous two victories this month, and if he wins with the chestnut colt today it's certain they'll be together at the Kentucky Derby early in May."

Alec turned from the screen to Henry, but his friend was watching Golden Vanity too intently to meet his gaze. Nino Nella was the rider whom Black Minx had taken through the rail last year in her first and only start in Florida as a two-year-old. Alec knew that a bad accident caused many a jockey to lose courage. That Nino Nella had come out of the hospital to ride so many winners, as the announcer had just pointed out, indicated that he had lost none of his nerve.

The picture had left Golden Vanity to pick up the other colts. All twelve were behind the post; some were already turned and coming into their starting-gate stalls. Others were being taken by their jockeys far up to the back turn. The television cameras followed them, trying to bring into view the majestic Sierra Madre Mountains beyond the backstretch. But only the lower slopes were visible because of the blanketing clouds.

"It's post time," the announcer said. "The track is fast. All colts carry the same weight of one hundred and eighteen pounds. They're starting one furlong—that's an eighth of a mile—behind the finish line of this mile track. That's Moon-struck now, going into his number three post position."

They watched the eastern colt and Henry grunted his approval. Moonstruck was a bay of moderate build but well balanced, strong to the fore and very muscular behind.

"Looks a little like our filly," Henry said.

Alec shook his head in disagreement. "He's lower set. I think he's definitely a sprinter. He'll get away fast with that driving equipment behind. But I don't think he'll be able to go the distance."

"He won some beautiful races last year at two," Henry said.

"But this is a mile and an eighth," Alec reminded him.

"Yeah, but still—" Henry paused, watching the number 6 colt approaching his stall.

The announcer was saying, "The number six horse going into the gate is another easterner, My Time. He's the second favorite. Last year My Time won . . ."

My Time was a big, dark colt, and his size would have impressed them more if they had not first seen Golden Vanity. He was a good sixteen hands, and as strong in line and body as the chestnut colt. My Time walked into his starting stall with a long reach, quick and racy. He looked as if he possessed a lot of speed.

"What'd he do last year?" Alec asked.

"No stake wins—but I think he needed a longer race. He'll have it today. He could win with no trouble at all."

All the colts were in the gate now. Alec and Henry sat awaiting the break, as tense as though they had saddled a colt for this race. The announcer's voice had stilled. He was waiting too. The heads of the horses could be seen within the wire-mesh doors of their individual gate stalls. There was no movement among them. The break would come any second.

Suddenly there was the sharp clang of the starting bell; the stall doors sprung open and a line of surging, bursting horse-flesh broke forward. For more than a hundred feet there could be seen only the straining heads of colts and jockeys. Then the picture shifted to a side view of the stretch run as the colts pounded past the grandstand for the first time.

The small eastern colt Moonstruck showed his nose in front as they swept by the judges' stand with a mile to go. The other colts were bunched, with little distance between any of them. Moonstruck increased his lead to a length, his short strides coming with amazing swiftness.

Without looking away from the picture, Alec said, "I told you he'd get away in front. He's low set for it. But watch him fold early."

"Not early," Henry said, "*if* he folds at all."

The colts were approaching the first turn. Moonstruck's lead was lengthening. He had three full lengths on the field now. His body was very low. He was stretched out all the way. He was flying!

Only when the field reached the turn did the line of colts behind Moonstruck break at all. Some of the jockeys pulled up, taking their horses behind others to save distance going around the turn.

Golden Vanity raced alongside Sadhu, who was on the rail. The favorite's chestnut body was stretched out, his strides coming fast and long. Nino Nella moved with him, his hands and feet going constantly, moving in rhythm with the big colt's strides. But Alec could see he wasn't pushing his mount. Not yet.

Henry said, "See what I meant when I said sometime ago

that Nino Nella was a 'huffle-scuffle' rider? He doesn't sit still a minute. Black Minx wouldn't take that kind of treatment from him."

Close behind Golden Vanity came the big eastern colt My Time. His dark face was just to the right of the chestnut's hindquarters. The rest of the field was close up. It was a mad surging pack with no colt yet out of the race, none giving way.

Moonstruck's short, fast strides were made for the turns. He stayed close to the rail, never lessening his speed. And when he came off the first turn he had put another length between him and the field. Into the backstretch they went.

Alec said, "They'll catch him now."

"No they won't."

Not another word was said. Neither knew which colt the other was rooting for. It didn't matter. The race was too exciting.

Moonstruck's strides didn't falter. He kept his four-length lead. But now the colts behind him were changing positions. My Time drew alongside Golden Vanity. Sadhu, on the rail, didn't fall back. The three colts were fighting a bitter duel without gaining on the small bay colt ahead of them. And from behind came another colt, a light gray, making his bid. He drew alongside My Time, stayed for a furlong, then dropped back again.

Halfway down the backstretch, Sadhu began losing ground. There was no way of telling if he had tired or if the pace of Golden Vanity and My Time had been stepped up. The jockeys moved with their mounts, straining with them. But neither of the two big colts shortened Moonstruck's lead.

Henry was on his feet now, his arms waving excitedly as he tried to root Moonstruck home. "Keep up there!" he shouted.

Alec, too, was on his feet, watching the small bay colt race for the back turn. He had thought Moonstruck a sprinter, but the colt now looked like a classic horse. He might go the distance. He might upset the favored Golden Vanity!

Moonstruck went into the far turn, still four lengths ahead. Behind him Golden Vanity moved ahead of My Time by inches. But Moonstruck maintained his long lead over both.

Once more the small bay colt took the turn with never a shortening stride. Now Golden Vanity was a length in front of My Time. His long strides took him away from the rail, seemingly losing more ground to Moonstruck. The flying leader came off the turn and entered the homestretch.

Alec's eyes followed him. With less than a quarter mile to go, Moonstruck's short strides were coming faster than ever. His jockey was asking for more speed and the colt was really turning it on.

Alec was watching Moonstruck so intently that he could think of nothing else until Henry said, "The chestnut, Alec!"

Golden Vanity came off the turn wide, his giant strides taking him almost to the center of the track. *Now* Nino Nella really was using his hands and heels to get more speed from the chestnut! Golden Vanity's strides came ever faster, then he was bearing down on Moonstruck with terrifying suddenness. The small bay colt was tiring, and Golden Vanity was coming down the stretch with a swiftness that was breathtaking.

He caught Moonstruck at the mile post, with a furlong to go. He passed the bay colt and opened daylight between them—one length, two, three, four, five, six, seven lengths. More than fifty yards from the finish wire, Nino Nella stopped using his hands and feet. He settled back in the saddle and came near standing in his stirrup irons as he slowed the chestnut colt. Yet Golden Vanity swept under the wire still a good five lengths ahead of Moonstruck.

Henry turned to Alec before sitting down again in his chair. "That chestnut really turned it on," he said.

Alec nodded. "He did that, all right. Golden Vanity looks like a great colt, Henry."

"But why did Nino Nella stand up before the finish?" Henry wondered.

"Maybe to save the colt," Alec said. "He knew he was going to win without any trouble."

Henry grunted. "And maybe because it made him and the colt look better."

The television cameras stayed on the colts as their jockeys slowed them going around the turn, and then singled out Golden Vanity as he made his way back toward the winner's circle.

"Who took third?" Henry asked.

"My Time. Sadhu was fourth," Alec said.

For a minute they listened to the announcer as he reviewed the race. Golden Vanity's time had equaled the track record despite his being pulled up by his jockey before the finish wire.

Alec was impressed. Turning away from the screen, he said, "That's amazing time for a three-year-old."

Henry shrugged his shoulders. "Yeah, but don't put too

much emphasis on it. In California they make track surfaces especially fast. I've seen too many horses who made good records out there come east and be beaten in races that were many seconds slower than their California times."

Alec studied Henry's face. "You're not underestimating Golden Vanity, are you?"

"No, of course not. He was by far the best in the race today. But I'm not going to come out and say he's an unbeatable whirlwind because of his fast time out there. He may be a Kentucky Derby winner and he may not. First I want to get a look at the other top three-year-olds; then I'll decide. Also, I'm not so sure right now that Golden Vanity can go a mile and a quarter."

"He went a mile and a furlong today," Alec said. "That means he had just another furlong to go for the Derby distance."

Henry smiled. "You know as well as I do it's that last eighth of a mile that counts in the Derby, Alec. I've seen lots of good colts stumble all over themselves trying to navigate it."

"But Golden Vanity's jock was pulling him up. He looked as though he had plenty of stamina left."

"That's exactly what I mean, Alec. It *looked* as if he had it, and maybe that's what they wanted us to think. I saw one or two things that make me think he might not be able to go a mile and a quarter."

"Perhaps you're right," Alec said. "But he looked awfully good to me."

"And maybe you're right," Henry relented. "Maybe he is another Morvich. Anyway, that's what the Californians will be shouting from the housetops now that he's won this race in record time. All I want to know is this—is he good enough to beat Silver Jet, Wintertime, and a few of the other top three-year-olds he'll have to contend with this year?" The trainer grinned. "Who knows? Maybe even Morvich couldn't have beaten 'em."

They watched Golden Vanity standing in the winner's circle, his great body sleek with sweat. He tossed his head and moved restlessly before the thousands of people gathered about the ring. The picture shifted to a tall young man who was about to be interviewed by the announcer.

"Congratulations, Mr. Graham," the announcer said. "How does it feel to own the winner of the Santa Anita Derby?"

The young man thrust his hands into the pockets of his checkered sports jacket. His thin, angular face bore a wide, good-natured smile. "Just wonderful," he said, "especially since Golden Vanity is the only horse I've ever owned."

"Your father-in-law, Mr. Frank Boyer, gave you the colt as a wedding present, didn't he?"

"Yes. At the time Golden Vanity was a yearling on Mr. Boyer's thoroughbred farm just north of Los Angeles. My father-in-law thought the colt was the best he'd ever bred. So he gave him to me as a present on the one condition that I'd have him trained and raced."

"And you're not sorry he made such a stipulation now, are you?" the announcer asked, smiling.

"No. No, indeed."

"And I suppose you'll be aiming for the Kentucky Derby next?"

"We certainly will. Golden Vanity earned his chance to start in that classic by winning today. But, of course, I'll leave all that up to my trainer, Ray Park."

The announcer called, "Ray Park, won't you step over here a moment?"

The trainer moved into view. He looked as young as Golden Vanity's owner.

"How do you feel about the colt's chances in the Kentucky Derby?" the announcer asked.

"He's an excellent colt," Park replied. "They'll have to break records to beat him."

"Then you think he's another Morvich?"

"I think he's better than Morvich. I think he's the finest colt ever bred in California. Furthermore, I'd like to add that I see no reason why California can't produce thoroughbreds as fine as those produced in Kentucky. And Golden Vanity is going to back me up in this." He smiled, and left.

The announcer next called, "Nino! Nino Nella. Will you please step over here a moment?"

The small jockey walked up to the announcer, his round full face turned to the camera. His bearing and attitude bespoke haughty arrogance, matching that of the golden chestnut colt he had ridden to victory.

"Nino, when did you feel you had the race won?"

"From the beginning," the jockey returned cockily.

"Never any doubt?"

"No. I ride him good."

The announcer smiled at the boy's brazen confidence. "We know that, Nino. You ride them all good."

"Sure," the jockey said.

"How about the Kentucky Derby, Nino? Will you be up on Golden Vanity?"

"That's up to Mr. Graham and Mr. Park," the boy replied, turning to the owner of Golden Vanity.

"He'll ride the colt," Mr. Graham said. "We wouldn't

break up a winning combination at this stage of the game."

A few moments later the program ended and Alec turned off the set. "Well," he said, "that's one of them." He thought again of the race, remembering the small, fast Moonstruck so far ahead of the field until the mile post. Their black filly might run much the same kind of race. She could race herself out, then go down beneath Golden Vanity's stretch run just as Moonstruck had done.

Henry said, "Next Saturday we'll get a line on Silver Jet. He'll race in the Flamingo Stakes in Florida."

The Kentucky Derby—*the Run for the Roses*—had already begun!

# *Derby Hopefuls*

## 9

During the following week the worst weather of the winter descended upon Hopeful Farm. Every day a cold rain fell, and all horses were kept in the barns. During this week too, four mares gave birth to their foals in the early hours of the morning. One other mare was due to foal any day or night, and required constant watching. Although Alex had sufficient help, the care and handling of mares, foals, yearlings, and stallions were under his supervision and occupied his every moment. He was too busy to give much thought to Black Minx and the Kentucky Derby.

Working along with him was Henry, who grumbled now and then about the inclement weather that forced him to keep his filly idle. He referred to the May classic only once. This was when he showed Alec a newspaper clipping which stated that more than one hundred three-year-olds had been nominated for the Kentucky Derby. It did not give the names of the eligibles whose owners had met the closing February deadline for entries in the classic. The list would be published later, and Black Minx's name would be there.

A change in the weather came early Saturday morning. It turned warm, and a hot sun helped to dry the sodden earth. The fields and paddocks were soft and muddy when the horses were turned out to enjoy the sun and get the kinks out of their legs. The new foals were kept in a sheltered paddock, where they could get some winter sunshine and yet avoid the hazards of a slippery field.

Alec made his rounds, carefully watching the mares—those who were barren, as well as those in foal. He handled the yearlings, grooming them and noticing that they were beginning to shed out their winter coats. He accepted this as an indication of an early spring. At eleven o'clock he brought in Satan and the Black from their paddocks. His next two hours were spent in the breeding shed.

After lunch he joined Henry and the black filly. Henry had her outside the barn and already saddled. She moved her feet restlessly in the mud, enjoying her first outing in a week.

"What'll it be today?" Alec asked as Henry boosted him up.

"Gallop two miles, easy."

Alec smiled, taking up the reins. "How else would she go but *easy*?"

Today was the third of March. Soon, Alec knew, Henry would be asking faster works from Black Minx. *Asking?* No, rather they'd trick the speed out of her, just as they had done a month ago.

With Henry leading the filly, they approached the stallion

barn. Alec saw Napoleon tied to the paddock fence and under saddle. "Are you riding with us, Henry?"

The trainer nodded without turning his head. "I thought I could use some exercise," he said.

Alec leaned forward to stroke the filly's neck. "That's hard to believe," he said. "You don't enjoy riding that much any more."

They reached Napoleon, and Henry, letting go of the filly, swung himself ponderously onto the old gray's back. Horse and rider grunted together until Henry got settled in his seat. He patted Napoleon. "Nothing better than a good stable pony," he said. "Nothin' worse than a bad one. C'mon, Nap. Let's go."

They started for the track, Black Minx stepping lightly over the soft ground and occasionally sending the mud flying from under her dancing feet. The gray gelding plodded beside her, making no pretense of enjoying himself but knowing there was nothing he could do about it.

Alec kept the filly in line and as quiet as possible. Turning in his saddle, he asked once more, "Why the ride, Henry?"

"I got a couple things in mind," the trainer finally answered. "First I want to go along with you to see how she acts on a muddy track. Then I thought that maybe a little company would get her to step up the pace on her own."

"You mean you think competition from other horses might cure her loafing? Then we wouldn't have to resort to any tricks?"

Henry shrugged his big shoulders. "Maybe so, Alec. I've seen a lot of horses who were lazy when worked alone, but showed up well when they had company." He paused. "Then again I've seen those who were real 'morning glories'—the kind who work sensationally alone but fall to pieces when they have company in the afternoon races. But I'm not certain about anything with this filly. She teaches me something new 'most every day."

Alec was silent during the rest of the ride to the track. Yet he turned in his saddle many times to study Henry's face. His friend never noticed Alec's glances, for Henry's head and eyes were downcast and he seemed to be in deep concentration. Alec watched him, wondering if Henry knew how much he valued his friendship. He must, of course. But it was one of those things in life which are seldom mentioned and all too often taken for granted.

Henry wasn't young any more, Alec knew. Many years ago Henry had given up the world of the thoroughbred. But the Black and Satan and now this filly had flung him back into the heat of it again. Yet Alec was certain that Henry was happy, for he had never really wanted to quit this life. So Henry was hanging on, his hair a little thinner and whiter each year, his eyes too often sad, his expression too grim. Sometimes, when Henry was most depressed, Alec knew his friend thought of retiring again, of never preparing another horse for another campaign . . . of just sitting back and relaxing. But this mood never lasted long. Henry would never quit, not as long as there was a horse for him to race. And now he had Black Minx, *his very own filly,* to get ready. There should be no holding him.

Reaching the track, Henry said, "I guess we'll be able to keep up with you. This old boy can still step along pretty good."

"I guess so," Alec returned. But he knew Henry was hoping that Napoleon's presence would urge the filly to extend herself of her own accord, so that Napoleon wouldn't be able to keep up with them.

They jogged to the post, Napoleon staying close to Black Minx and ignoring the sharp swerving of her body against him. The old horse had spent too many hours with the Black and Satan to be bothered unduly by this youngster. Henry patted him fondly as they turned around.

"Okay. Let's go head on head. I'll keep on the outside."

As soon as Alec gave her rein, Black Minx moved into a gallop. Napoleon plunged alongside, having no trouble at all in keeping up with her. They made the first turn and entered the backstretch.

Henry watched the filly. "Let her go ahead, if she wants to," he said.

"She doesn't want to," Alec returned, clucking to her, urging her.

- He was right. The only effect Napoleon's presence had on her was that she constantly turned her small head toward him, not to nip but seemingly to carry on a conversation with him. She actually neighed, snorted, and whinnied while they circled the track.

Alec said glumly, "She's a great one, she is. I can just see her trying to start a conversation with Golden Vanity as he booms past her in the Derby."

Henry glanced angrily at Alec. He hadn't thought the remark funny at all. His face grim, he rode Napoleon alongside the filly for another mile. Then, going around the track for the last time, he clucked to the old gray horse and began moving ahead.

Alec watched Napoleon go out a length, then started urging the filly to step up her gallop. There was no response.

Napoleon could have lapped her for all the interest she showed. Perhaps she didn't care. Or perhaps she sensed what they were trying to do. At any rate, she never once moved out of her slow, effortless gallop.

Coming down the homestretch for the last time, Henry slowed Napoleon, allowing Black Minx to catch up again. His face was grimmer, more disappointed, than Alec had ever seen it. Henry had sincerely expected the filly to extend herself a little with Napoleon running beside her.

The trainer didn't meet Alec's gaze. Instead he concentrated on Black Minx's feet, watching her strides carry her over the heavy mud. No doubt about it, she could handle herself well on a muddy track.

They slowed their mounts at the end of the two-mile gallop. When Alec had Black Minx in a jog, he said, "She seems to take to the mud, all right. But you know, Henry, her feet barely touch it before she has them up again. She acts as though she doesn't want to get them dirty. It's just about what we should expect of her, I guess."

"She won't be able to keep so clean if she lets a field of horses get in front of her," Henry said, anger and disappointment in his voice.

Never before had Alec heard him talk that way about the filly. Alec was disturbed but he kept quiet, knowing there was nothing he could say that would help.

They were almost at the barns when Henry said, "Well, we know we can get the speed out of her another way." He sounded more like himself again, but Alec recognized the feigned lightness of his voice.

"Sure we can, Henry. It doesn't matter how we get it out of her just as long as we get it." He wasn't kidding himself any more than Henry. It did matter. He *wanted* the filly to respond in the face of competition, to have her sire's will to win. But he knew this was foolish optimism. Reaching down to Black Minx's chest, he removed a piece of mud that had already caked in the hot sun.

Henry said, "It's all right to trick her into running as long as she doesn't *run herself out* in the race. I got to figure a way of conserving some of her energy."

There it was out in the open—the problem of rating the filly during the running of a race. It was the same problem Alec himself had considered some nights ago while working on his field chart. He hadn't come up with any answers. Would Henry?

Black Minx swerved but he brought her back in line. He turned to Henry. He wanted to help. "Do you think it would be possible to take the bit away from her when she needs rest, and then give it back to her when we want her to move on again?"

Henry shook his head. "That might work when we start breezing her and have all the time in the world. But it wouldn't work in a race, when every second counts. She'd fight before the bit could be taken from her, and besides getting no rest would lose plenty of ground. Also, she might get wise to what's being done. No, once she takes the bit it's best to leave her alone."

Upon reaching the filly's barn, they unsaddled her. Alec put a blanket over her warm body. A light breeze blew and he thought he detected the scent of new grass from the fields. It was only early March, so he must be mistaken. Yet he could feel something in the air—perhaps it was the languid stir of an early spring.

They were walking Black Minx and Napoleon, cooling them off, when Alec said, "Henry, I wonder if we could keep her right behind the front runners? If she couldn't get past them, she couldn't run herself out."

Henry thought for a moment. Then, "That might do it," he replied eagerly. "It just could." He paused. "It would take delicate handling and fine riding so nobody would get hurt. Yet I might find a jockey who could do it." He stopped again, this time studying Alec's face. Finally he said, "All the time you've been saying *we*, Alec. You didn't mean you were thinking about riding her in the Derby? You wouldn't want to leave the farm, even for a short while, would you?"

"If you want me to, I'll ride her," Alec said.

Henry turned away, and they continued walking Black Minx and Napoleon. "I want you, all right," the trainer said softly, and the grimness was gone from his face.

# *The Flamingo*

## 10

Later that same afternoon Alec and Henry sat before the television set, watching the ceremonies that were taking place at Hialeah Park, Florida. The running of the Flamingo Stakes was an important and colorful event, and the track management was making good use of its television time before the horses went to the post.

On the screen a large party of Seminole Indians was parading within the track's infield. Men, women, and children, dressed in flowing capes and skirts, walked with stately dignity past the grandstand. Then they turned and went back up the infield to sit down upon the grass.

Alec didn't pay much attention to them. He was anxious for the race to start. Now that he had told Henry he would ride Black Minx in the Derby he was more interested than ever in watching the colts he'd be up against. He turned to Henry but his friend's eyes were closed and, like Alec, he was taking no interest in the pre-race ceremonies.

Henry had said nothing more about Alec's decision to ride in the Derby. Nor had Alec expected him to go into it more fully. Again, it was one of those things that needed no discussion between them. Henry knew that Alec was most happy here at the farm, away from the racetrack with all its pulsating drama, excitement, and glamor. Therefore, Henry realized that Alec would be riding the filly in the Derby only because he had confidence in his ability to get the best out of her and because Henry needed him.

Henry opened his eyes, found Alec's gaze upon him, and asked, "Are the Seminoles still parading?"

Alec glanced at the screen. "They've just about finished," he said.

Henry grunted, closing his eyes again. "The track's publicity department considers it colorful stuff for Flamingo Day, and the crowd thinks the Seminoles are a bunch of wild Indians from the Everglades. Nothin' wild about them except that they come from the wilds of a tourist trap called Musa Village just off one of Florida's most traveled highways. They get paid for coming over to the track on Flamingo Day and putting on their act."

Alec's gaze returned to the screen. "Nevertheless, it *is* colorful," he said.

The picture shifted from the Seminole Indians to the crowded grandstand, the cement apron in front of it, and then to the clubhouse and bleachers.

"The season's largest crowd is here today," the announcer told his television audience. "More than thirty thousand people are now awaiting the running of the Flamingo Stakes."

Henry opened his eyes.

White shirts and blouses dominated the color scheme; the day was apparently hot. As a protection against the sun, many of the fans standing before the grandstand and sitting in the bleachers wore hats made from newspapers.

The television cameras left the packed thousands to show the grass and small infield lake which lent the only cool note to an otherwise sweltering day. Five hundred long-legged flamingos had been chased from the lake and were being herded together. A crew of ten men moved the rare, beautiful birds across the grass in the direction of the stands.

The announcer said, "The parade of the flamingos is about to begin. This show is put on only once a year, the day of the running of the Flamingo Stakes."

The birds paraded before the stands, their handlers chasing them until finally they rose in hurried flight. The screen was filled with flapping wings, long extended necks, and trailing legs. Finally the birds descended and scampered back to their unmolested haunts in the infield lake. The show was over but the cameras remained focused on the flamingos until a roar from the crowd announced the arrival of the horses on the track. Quickly the picture shifted to the post parade.

For the first time Henry showed some interest in the proceedings. He pushed himself forward in his chair, one large hand covering his jaw. "There's Silver Jet," he said.

There were seven colts going to the post but Alec watched only Silver Jet, for here was the top-rated three-year-old in the country and the early favorite to win the Kentucky Derby. He saw a well-finished gray with long flowing mane and tail. The colt was tall but not oversized, and his walk was easy and swinging. He wore blinkers and his head was small, sitting well into a short, muscular neck. Although Silver Jet had style he showed none of the high-headed air of arrogance which had so marked Golden Vanity, the winner of the Santa Anita Derby. Instead he moved in an unruffled yet confident way.

Henry said, "He's wearing bandages in front."

Alec noted the bandaged legs from knees to fetlocks. "Do you think he's been hurt?"

"No. They wouldn't be running him if he was. I suppose they're just being careful."

"Has he raced much in Florida?"

"Three times," Henry replied. "Won 'em all, easy."

The announcer said, "They're asking just two questions about today's race. How far will Silver Jet win? And will he break the Flamingo record of one minute, forty-eight and one-fifth seconds?"

Alec turned to Henry. "That time is one-fifth of a second faster than Golden Vanity won at Santa Anita."

"Florida tracks are hard and fast too," Henry said, without taking his eyes off the screen. "They're not easy on a horse's legs."

The colts were going into the starting gate.

"That's Danny Seymour up on Silver Jet," Alec said.

The picture showed a close-up of the gate and Alec had no trouble recognizing the mature, wizened face of the veteran jockey who sat on the back of the gray colt in the number 2 starting stall. He watched Seymour's quiet skill in handling Silver Jet as the colt became uneasy.

The starter's assistants had the last horse in the gate now. Any second they'd be off. Alec kept his eyes on Seymour and the gray colt. He noticed that Silver Jet was still moving within his narrow stall. Seymour was trying to quiet him down. An assistant starter straddled the partition between the stalls in an attempt to help the jockey. Alec wondered that Silver Jet could be so docile on his way to the post and yet so fractious in the gate.

"Is he always that way?" he asked Henry.

"No, not quite as bad as he is today. Usually he acts up a little in the gate, then settles down fast. He's quick in the break. He likes to run in front or up near the front, anyway. Same type of runner as Golden Vanity. Their meeting, whenever it comes, should be a good show."

Silver Jet settled down in his stall.

"The start will come now," Alec said. "They're all quiet."

But simultaneously with the opening of the stall doors and the clang of the starting bell, Silver Jet reared, his head turned sideways. In a fraction of a second Alec saw Seymour straighten him out. Nevertheless, Silver Jet broke from the gate with his head still partly turned to one side. Seymour had lost his stirrups in all the excitement and was trying to find the irons again as Silver Jet set out after the field. Recovering his stirrups, Seymour sat down to ride.

As the field approached the first turn Silver Jet was five lengths behind, yet Seymour made no move to hurry his mount.

Alec said quietly, "Watch him, Henry. Lots of riders would try to make up all that lost ground in the first quarter of a mile. But not Seymour. He's keeping his head. He'll let the colt get warmed to his work, and then move him through the stretch."

Henry nodded in agreement but didn't take his eyes off the race.

Alec ignored the front runners. He watched Silver Jet. He watched Dan Seymour. Here was an experienced jockey, aged compared to the eighteen-year-old Nino Nella. Now he was sitting tight over his colt's neck, making no move with hands or feet or whip to hurry him. The horses swept around the first turn and into the backstretch, and Silver Jet was still a good five lengths behind the bunched field.

Henry swayed in his chair as though to urge Dan Seymour to move his colt. But the jockey remained quiet in his saddle. For a second Alec visualized Nino Nella instead of Dan Seymour astride Silver Jet. He knew, from having watched the Santa Anita Derby, that Nino Nella would be working his hands and feet all the way in an attempt to catch up with the field.

The gray colt caught up with two lagging colts by the middle of the backstretch. It wasn't that Seymour was moving Silver Jet faster, merely that the two colts were tiring. Saving precious ground, Seymour squeezed Silver Jet between them. Only when the gray colt's blinkered head emerged from the narrow hole and he was free and clear did Alec glance quickly at Henry to find the trainer's eyes meeting his.

In saving his colt a few feet of extra ground, Seymour had taken a long gamble on his ability to slip between the two lagging horses instead of going around them. It had been an example of fine riding, with no loud cries of "Coming through!" or pumping of hands and legs. The jockey had done it skillfully, easily, with his head never leaving the gray's neck, his hands barely moving.

Alec and Henry saw immediately why Seymour had used the "hole." He was on the rail and taking Silver Jet *inside* the colts ahead whose speed caused them to bear out going around the last turn. Only then did they see Dan Seymour's hand move. The jockey brought the whip down once, hard, against the colt.

Silver Jet responded with a burst of speed that took him past all but one of the colts. He hugged the rail, Seymour sitting tight and unmoving in his saddle again. He came off the turn only two lengths behind the brown colt who was leading. With less than a quarter of a mile to go, Seymour used his whip once more. Again the colt responded with terrific speed. He caught up with the brown colt easily; then he was out in front, racing alone, and there was no further need for Seymour to urge him to greater speed. Beautiful and swift, he came down the homestretch all by himself, his strides ever lengthening. Gray mane and tail billowed in the wind. As he passed beneath the wire the tremendous crowd was on its feet paying noisy homage to him.

Alec said, "Seymour is stingy with his whip. He uses it only when he thinks he needs it. He's one of the best hand riders in the business. He can do more with his hands alone than any other jockey can do with a dozen whips and kicks."

The time of the race was announced as 1:48 3/5. Silver Jet had failed to break the record, and his time was one-fifth of a second slower than Golden Vanity's at Santa Anita over the same distance.

"If he hadn't been left at the post, he might have broken the record," Henry said. "Like I mentioned before, he runs best up front."

"How do you like him compared to Golden Vanity?" Alec asked.

Henry shrugged his shoulders. "When they meet, something is goin' to give."

"Seriously, Henry, how do they shape up in your opinion?" Alec persisted.

"We got some other colts to watch before Derby time. No sense in going out on the limb for any one of 'em now, Alec."

"But I think you like Silver Jet better than Golden Vanity."

"What makes you say that?"

"Well, the fast time, for one thing," Alec said.

"But he went a fifth of a second slower than Golden Vanity over the same distance," Henry replied.

"I know. But as you pointed out, he was left at the post. If he hadn't been, his time would have been faster by at least a fifth of a second." Alec paused. "And there's something else. Silver Jet was carrying a hundred and twenty-six pounds today, the same weight all the colts will be carrying in the Derby. When Golden Vanity won at Santa Anita he carried only a hundred and eighteen pounds. Put all this together and you come up with Silver Jet beating Golden Vanity in the Kentucky Derby. Right, Henry?"

"Maybe," Henry replied. "Just maybe. Anyway, it's a long time from the first Saturday in March to the first Saturday in May."

The announcer had the owner of Silver Jet before the television cameras. They saw Tom Flint's towering frame and they watched his broad, beaming face as he acknowledged the congratulations of the Governor of Florida, who was making the cup presentation.

"Sure I was thrilled. Who wouldn't be?" Tom Flint said.

"No, there's nothing wrong with his forelegs. We were just being careful. He's raced a lot down here. We're giving him a rest until the Wood Memorial in New York next month."

"And after that?" the announcer asked, smiling.

Tom Flint placed a big hand on the man's shoulder. "Then we'll be heading for the bluegrass country. Today my colt earned his plane ticket to the Kentucky Derby."

A few minutes later the announcer had Dan Seymour before the camera. The jockey stood there as quietly as he had sat in the saddle during the running of the race. His small, drawn face was turned to the announcer as he rapidly answered the questions put to him. He was completely at ease despite the ceremonies and the acclaim of the crowd. He had been through this before in his many years of riding.

"No, I didn't have my feet in the stirrups when the gate opened. It wasn't anybody's fault that I was left behind. The starter didn't get a chance to know Silver Jet was going up." He smiled. "I didn't, either."

"Did the colt ever do that before with you?"

"No. He acts up a little but today he seemed more anxious than ever to get away. There's no explanation as to why it happened. It just did. I got him down and we came out. That's all."

"How'd the colt react to running behind? We all know he likes to be up front."

"Naturally, he runs best up front," Seymour replied. "But he gave me no trouble while we were behind. Like any front runner he had to be shaken up with the whip going into the back turn. But he responded quickly and once he got up near the front there was no stopping him. I had nothing to do after that."

"How do you feel your chances are in the Kentucky Derby, Dan?"

"Good as anybody's," the jockey said. "But anything can happen in that race."

When the program ended, Alec and Henry left the attic together. Going down the stairs Alec said, "Still think we're going to win the Derby, Henry?"

"Like Dan Seymour just pointed out, *anything can happen in the Kentucky Derby, Alec.*"

# Spring Breezes

## 11

In reading Sunday's newspapers Alec and Henry learned that their great interest in the Flamingo Stakes had caused them to overlook another preparatory race for the Kentucky Derby, which had taken place the same day. It was the Louisiana Derby at New Orleans.

Alec didn't feel that it was an important race, but Henry reminded him that back in 1924 Black Gold had won this race and had then gone on to win the Kentucky Derby. They shouldn't ignore it or its results, particularly since Henry liked the winner.

The newspaper story telling of the race read:

> A big gal from the wrong side of the tracks beat the colts in Saturday's running of the Louisiana Derby.
>
> Lady Lee, who was at New Orleans only

because her owner and trainer didn't feel that she was up to handling Silver Jet and other top colts in Florida, came down the homestretch to win by two lengths over the favored Sweep. The rangy brown filly's victory was most impressive, for she was in ninth place entering the last furlong of the mile-and-an-eighth feature. Her Kentucky Derby stock was boosted by her clocking of 1:49 1/5, which compares favorably with Silver Jet's 1:48 3/5 in winning the Flamingo. Her time was all the more impressive because the track was good but not fast.

It has been said that to win a classic race such as the Kentucky Derby a horse must have a fashionable pedigree. Lady Lee doesn't qualify since her sire (Tim S.) and her dam (Mae Lee) are not considered "fashionable" by those who set equine standards. Moreover, neither her sire nor her dam accomplished any notable achievements on the track during their racing days.

But many who saw Lady Lee win on Saturday claim she is as good a filly as there is in the country, and better than most of the top colts. She is large and well put together. She's tough and seems to like distance. So although it is well known that any filly is a downright uncertain proposition in the spring, especially so in a classic distance race such as the Kentucky Derby, it just might be possible that Lady Lee will show her

down-trodden heels to the colts of more
fashionable pedigree.

Lady Lee's next engagement will be in the
first Experimental Handicap in New York
on April 9.

Finishing the story, Alec asked, "What colts will she meet
in the Experimental?"

"There's no way of telling how many will go to the post.
Eclipse and Wintertime should be in there. Both have been
wintering in the Carolinas."

"That means spring isn't too far off, Henry."

"No—or the Derby either."

"And you like Eclipse and Wintertime, don't you?" Alec
asked.

"I think their chances of doing something in the Derby
are as good as Silver Jet's and Golden Vanity's, if that's what
you mean. Maybe better," Henry added hastily.

"Why?"

"Because I'm of the school that doesn't believe in the winter racing of three-year-olds. It's too tough to keep a young
colt at the peak of his form from February until May."

"Some of the winter-raced colts have gone on to win the
Kentucky Derby," Alec reminded him. "And Silver Jet and
Golden Vanity will be taking their rests now. They won't be
racing again until the last of April, just before Derby week."

"I know," Henry grumbled. "I'm just prejudiced in favor
of the way Eclipse and Wintertime are being trained.
They're being taken along slowly until they're fit and ready
to go. If that happens by the first Saturday in May it's soon
enough."

"You forgot to include Black Minx," Alec said, smiling.

"Black Minx then," Henry repeated.

The next few nights, like the days, were busy ones for Alec. Three mares foaled on successive nights. Two of the mares were owned by outside patrons, and the sires of the foals resided in Kentucky. But the third mare belonged to them and she foaled a filly by the Black.

Alec watched the filly struggle to her feet shortly after birth. He was overjoyed that this one was a filly, the first filly by the Black to be born at Hopeful Farm. He wiped her nostrils clean and attended the mare. After the filly nursed he left the stall. He stood outside watching her and wondering what she'd be like when she grew up. She would have the gray coat of her dam. Her head and body seemed a little coarse right now but in time she might change to look more like *him.*

*Sires are only half,* he reminded himself. *None of them can be the Black all over again.*

As Henry had said time and time again, all they could ever do here at Hopeful Farm was to buy the best-blooded mares they could afford and mate them intelligently. After that they would give the foals the finest care men and money could provide, and finally the best of training. They were expensive methods and wouldn't always pay off. But there was no other way to run Hopeful Farm or any stock farm.

Alec left the foaling barn. Each new foal was different. Each required his own special way of handling. And it would be the same later on, as he was finding out now with Black Minx, when they became old enough to race. Henry once said, Alec remembered, that this special handling and training of the Black's colts and fillies was exactly what made it all so exciting and worthwhile. How right he was! Hopeful

Farm wasn't the end of the road for any of them—for himself or Henry, for the Black or Satan. Actually, it was just the
beginning of new adventures!

During the following week, the third in March, the wind
shifted to the south, bringing with it the early spring Alec
had sought. Every day the sun shone hot, and Alec was able
to see, in paddocks and fields, the first green tinge. Most certainly he could smell the grass starting to grow again. And
there was no doubt that the towering tulip tree behind the
stallion barn was budding. Or that there was a sudden influx
of birds in fields and bushes. All week long, as he went about
his work, he watched the flight of the birds through the
silky spring air.

Early Saturday morning Alec held the filly's bridle while
Henry saddled her. "We got what you wanted, Henry—an
easy winter. Now spring is here," he said excitedly.

Henry's eyes never left the girth strap he was tightening.
"I know," he replied. "She's as hard as I could want her.
Now we'll start her real work."

"Today?"

"Yeah. Come on. Get up now." He boosted Alec into the
saddle, and led the filly up the lane. "From here on we get
real serious," he added.

The track was soft but not slippery. There were no pud-
dles, for the sandy loam had absorbed all moisture from the
previous week's rain. Black Minx stepped lightly on the
track, more restless than usual, as if she too knew that spring
was at hand.

Alec held her close. "What'll it be, Henry?"

"Breeze a half in about fifty seconds. Then gallop out the
rest of the mile."

Black Minx tossed her head, but Henry held on to her bridle.

Alex said, "I doubt that I can rate her, Henry. When she takes the bit she'll work the limit of her speed." He knew the difference between a work and a breeze, but the filly didn't. And there was no way of teaching her. When Henry called for "breezing" he wanted his horse to move fast, but at the same time to be held under a snug hold and not allowed to reach the limit of its speed. When he called for a "work" he wanted his horse to go at top speed, with urging if necessary.

How could breezes and works be specified in the training of Black Minx?

Henry said, "Let her have the bit but take it away from her several times during the half-mile. That'll slow her down."

"I don't think it's a good idea. She'll get wise to what we're doing if we try that game very often. It'll ruin everything."

"Maybe so," Henry agreed. "Then take the bit from her before reaching the half. Do it at about the three-eighths post. That should make her finish the half-mile about right."

Alec nodded. "Let go of the bridle, Henry."

Henry stepped back. Although Alec kept the filly still, he was alert to the moving of her mouth. He wanted her to break with the bit between her teeth. That's the way it would be in a race. He gave her a little more freedom of rein but kept control. She started toying with the bit, and he felt her teeth on it. He glanced at Henry and nodded.

Leaning forward he whispered softly, "Whoa, girl. Still now." His hands turned the bit over to her. Her ears pitched forward. Her body quivered in excitement as she moved the bit.

Alec knew she was getting ready to bolt with him. He encouraged her recklessness still more by whispering again, "Steady, girl. Whoa." Her ears flicked back at his words, and then pitched forward again.

Suddenly she was off, the bit between her teeth! Alec moved forward, giving her freedom of movement. But his hands were now working in a feigned attempt to stop her. And he did not forget to repeat the command "Whoa!" in her ear every few seconds.

She streaked down the stretch, and as she entered the turn, her small head was stretched out, pulling the reins tight. Alec smiled as he shifted his weight into the turn with her. He was careful to see that no hasty, abrupt movement of his hands would dislodge the bit from between her teeth. He pressed his head hard against her straining neck, and continued to plead with her to stop.

The rail and posts sped by. How this filly could run, when she wanted to! Her light feet barely touched the ground before they were up again, driving her on. In his excitement Alec almost forgot to cry "Whoa!" It was so natural for him to urge and encourage his mount to greater speed. So strange to keep such a tight hold on the reins, to call out in protest of her speed. Such a bewildering way to get the filly to extend herself!

Only when they were in the middle of the back turn did he remember Henry's instructions. As they passed the three-eighths pole, Alec moved his hands carefully. Black Minx fought him desperately as he tried to get the bit loose. She tossed her head, swerving across the track, not caring where she went. Alec succeeded in getting the bit away from her in time to straighten her out before she went completely off the track. She slowed down as soon as he had control again. Alec took her down the homestretch and around the oval again, finishing out the mile in a gallop as Henry had wanted.

On their way back to the barn, Henry said, "Her fighting and swerving when you take the bit from her is just another reason we won't be able to try that kind of thing in a race. She'd get so mad she'd move right into other horses without ever seeing 'em." He paused. "The only thing we can do, Alec, is to follow your suggestion. Let her take the bit. Then try to keep her behind the pacesetters so she can't move ahead until you're ready for her to go all out. As I said before, it'll take mighty delicate handling. I'm glad you're goin' to be up on her. I wouldn't want to see anyone else try it."

Alec said, "It looks as though breezing her is out, too. We'll have to continue working her as we did today."

"I guess so. She's ready to be set down anyway. It won't hurt her, if we're careful not to go at it too often. We'll continue to do a lot of galloping."

In the next day's newspapers they read the names of the three-year-olds that had been nominated to run in the Kentucky Derby. Henry studied the list carefully, but Alec took only enough time from his farm duties to note that Black Minx's name was included. He remembered too that more than one hundred colts, geldings, and fillies had been nominated for the Derby of the previous year, and that only fourteen had actually gone to the post. How many of these one hundred and thirty-four hopefuls would face the starter this year? Would Black Minx be among them?

With spring already here, there would be more three-year-olds ready to go, more preparatory races to watch. Would Eclipse and Wintertime come forward to earn their share in the Kentucky Derby spotlight? Within a couple of weeks those two colts could be racing, and both of them would probably encounter Silver Jet and Golden Vanity before the Derby. The spotlight would get smaller and smaller until finally on the first Saturday in May only one colt would be favored by its brilliance. Or maybe there would be a *filly* instead of a colt in the Derby winner's circle. Alec didn't have Lady Lee in mind when he considered this. He was thinking of a black filly who liked to do things her own way.

# *The Experimental Handicaps*

## 12

By the first week of April, Henry was giving Black Minx speed works of three-quarters of a mile. He began clocking her, too, and although he never told Alec her time, it was obvious that he was pleased. He continued ordering slow gallops around a mile to two miles long, but frequently work days were postponed altogether. Often, too, he had Alec simply walk the filly about the track.

Alec did only as he was instructed and never queried Henry about the training schedule. He knew his friend was involved with one of the most exacting tasks a trainer could have—that of getting a horse ready to win its first start of the year at a mile or over. The job would have been difficult even with a placid, reliable horse. In that case Henry could have worked out a training schedule beforehand and maintained it. But he couldn't train Black Minx by the book. Her nervous, fretful temperament caused Henry to change his scheduled workouts regularly. And when he had the filly walk around the track rather than gallop or work fast as planned, Alec knew he was afraid the filly was getting ready too soon and might go stale before her big race.

Black Minx never blew or sweated profusely, even after her fast works. She had grown and filled out more during the long months Alec had been riding her. Her coat, too— short and glossy black—reflected her present good condition.

Alec realized that Henry had done a remarkable job in curing Black Minx of her bad stable manners and in making her what she was today. The gamble was whether or not she would hold her condition as her works became longer and faster. And how far could she hold her speed? Alec thought she'd go a mile, but he wasn't certain about her ability to go a mile and a quarter. The last quarter-mile of the Kentucky Derby called for more than stamina. It called for heart and courage, and the will to win. In these the filly was lacking.

Henry too must have had his doubts, for late one afternoon Alec found him reading the list of eligibles for the Kentucky Oaks. The Oaks was the "Derby for Fillies," and was raced the day before the Kentucky Derby at Churchill Downs. Fifty-six fillies had been nominated by their owners. Lady Lee was on the list. So was Black Minx. In most cases, a filly nominated for the Kentucky Derby was also nominated for the Kentucky Oaks. The reason was simple. Nomination fees were only fifty dollars for each race, payable in February, and the owners had until the first week in May to decide whether to enter their fillies in the Derby or the Oaks.

Alec knew Henry was asking himself the same question that every owner of a filly mulled over at this time of the year and would continue to do until May.

*Will the colts and the distance be too much for her in the Derby?
In the Oaks she'll be racing against her own sex. The distance will
be but a mile and a sixteenth, and much more to her liking. To
start her in the Oaks will cost me only two hundred and fifty dollars, but the Derby means shelling out a thousand to start her.
Sure, there's almost a hundred thousand waiting for the Derby
winner. But maybe she won't win. There's close to twenty-five
thousand dollars waiting for the filly who wins the Oaks. She's got
a better chance of copping it. Twenty-five thousand dollars can buy
a lot of hay. Yeah, I'd better think more about the Oaks and less
about the Derby. But not right now. I got a lot of time to make up
my mind. And there's no race like the Derby. I'd sure like to see her
in the Derby. Well, if she looks right, maybe . . . yes, maybe. I'll
let it go at that for now.*

And that was the reason Henry only shrugged his shoulders when Alec asked him if he was considering the Kentucky Oaks for Black Minx instead of the Derby.

Three more foals were born early the first week in April,
and another was due on the fourth. These foals, together
with breeding operations being in full swing, kept Alec too
busy to think more about the Kentucky Derby or the Kentucky Oaks. But with all his help—Henry, his father, and the
three hired men—the work went smoothly. He was glad the
foals were arriving on schedule. One more was to come
soon. Then no others would be due until late May, allowing
him time to spend the last week in April and the first in May
at Churchill Downs. His father and the hired men would
take care of the farm operations during his brief absence.

Wednesday afternoon Henry restricted Black Minx's outing on the track to a three-mile walk. Later, in the barn, Alec
and Henry discussed the Experimental Handicap to be raced
in New York within an hour's time.

Henry said, "It'll be the first race for Eclipse and Wintertime."

"How'd they winter?" Alec wanted to know.

"Good, from all I hear. Wintertime is reported to have done a mile in a minute and forty seconds on the farm track before being shipped to New York. But they say he didn't grow as much as was expected during the winter. He still stands at a little over fifteen hands. But he's filled out sidewise and developed more muscle."

"And Eclipse?" Alec asked.

Henry's eyes lighted. "There's a colt!" he said.

Alec smiled. "Sure, I know. You like him and he was second only to Silver Jet as a two-year-old. But how does he look now? How'd he winter?"

"My friends at the track say he never looked better," Henry confided. "He's sleek and in high flesh. Grew some, too, standing a scant sixteen hands. And solid, they say. He'd been turned out for a month in North Carolina. He rested and loosened up after all his hard racing last year. He started galloping the last of January and got on the farm track every day. He was shipped to New York a couple of weeks ago."

"And how's he been working?"

"Get this, Alec," Henry almost whispered. "He did six furlongs the other morning in a minute and eleven seconds! And my friends say that they were impressed even more by the easy way he did it. Just as smooth as silk in action. No doubt about it," Henry concluded. "He's fit and ready to run."

"Then you think he'll have a good chance of winning today's race, even though he'll be carrying top weight of a hundred and twenty-five pounds?"

"Sure I do," Henry said emphatically. "He shouldn't have

any trouble at all with the rest of 'em."

Alec considered the distance of the race. It was only six furlongs, three-quarters of a mile. He thought it too short a race for Eclipse. And certainly it wouldn't give them much of an idea of what the same horses might do over a longer distance. Well, they'd have just such a race in little more than a week. The Experimental Handicap was raced at two distances. Number One was today's race at six furlongs. Number Two would be held on the fourteenth and would be run over a mile and a sixteenth, a more revealing test for Kentucky Derby eligibles.

Alec turned to Henry, who was about finished with his grooming of Black Minx. "Don't forget Lady Lee will be in there today," he said. "And she'll have only a hundred and eight pounds on her back."

"Yeah, I know," Henry said.

"I'm surprised she wasn't given a longer rest after all her winter racing."

"I'm not," Henry said.

"Why?"

"Her owner and trainer probably figure they've side-stepped the top colts long enough," Henry explained. "They want to find out just what they've got in their filly. So they'll race her in both Experimentals and a few other races as well. If they find that there are a couple of colts around that she just can't beat they'll save her for the Kentucky Oaks and other filly races, and skip the Derby."

Alec nodded. "I see what you mean," he said. "And today she sets out by meeting Eclipse and Wintertime."

"Yeah." Henry left the filly's stall after glancing at his watch. "It's not long before post time. Let's get to the television set."

They started down the corridor but didn't get very far before Jinx, one of the broodmare men, appeared in the doorway. He called to them, "That young mare is foaling, and it looks like she might need some help!"

They broke into a run, Alec saying, "You go watch the race, Henry. I'll stay with the mare."

"Not on your life," Henry said. "It's her first foal. The race can wait."

It took thirty minutes for the young mare to foal and become acquainted with her first son. They stayed close to her, making certain she realized what had happened and that this foal was hers. Finally she accepted the colt and the danger of her injuring him was over. She was an outside mare and the sire of the colt was a Kentucky stallion, but Alec and Henry treated mare and foal as they would their own. When they left the stall, Jinx was instructed to stay there a little longer.

They reached the television set only in time to catch the acclaim that was being given to the winner of the Experimental Handicap. A tall rangy filly stood in the winner's circle with flowers about her neck. It was *Lady Lee!*

The announcer stood beside her, talking to a small man whose round face was beaming.

"Sure, it's wonderful!" he told the announcer. "I never thought I'd own a horse like her. Not one that could beat Eclipse by three lengths and Wintertime by four. No, sir, I never did!"

Alec glanced at Henry. Lady Lee had beaten Eclipse soundly, and Wintertime had been still another length behind! He turned back to the screen.

Lady Lee's owner was saying, his face shining more than ever, "Oh, I'm just a little guy in racing. The Kentucky Derby? Well, I can hope, can't I?" He laughed. "I'm still too nervous over winning this race. Why, she was in front all the way! Did you see her? They never got close!"

At the close of the interview Alec turned off the set. "She must be a lot better filly than I'd thought."

Henry grunted. He had been so certain Eclipse would win.

Alec continued, "You said last winter you liked her chances in the Derby."

"I was only guessing," Henry replied. "But from today's race it looks like maybe I was right. We'll know more when she goes a mile and a sixteenth against Eclipse. If she should trim him over that distance, well . . ."

"Things are getting hot," Alec said as they left the attic.

On Saturday, April 14, Alec and Henry were back at the television set, awaiting the running of Experimental Handicap Number Two. This should be a race to remember, and one with a direct bearing on the coming Derby. Anxiously and with little conversation between them, they whiled away the minutes before the horses appeared on the screen.

The horses were on their way to the post. There were seven in the parade, but Alec and Henry had eyes for only three of them. The announcer, too, realized that this race would be strictly a three-horse battle among Lady Lee, Eclipse, and Wintertime. He therefore was giving his time and attention to them.

Lady Lee dominated the screen as he spoke of her achievements. She was very tall for a filly, almost sixteen hands, and light for her height. Rangy was the word for Lady Lee, for her long, thin legs carried a long, thin body. She was light brown and her head was as angular as the rest of her. Now, as she moved into a slow gallop, Alec and Henry noted the smooth strides which were in sharp contrast to her ungainliness at a walk.

The announcer was saying, "Lady Lee rocketed into the Kentucky Derby picture last week when she stunned a crowd of more than forty thousand people here with a walloping three-length victory over the favorite, Eclipse, who was and still is, despite the upset, one of the top favorites to win the Kentucky Derby early next month. However, if he loses again today to Lady Lee it will be another story.

"The overwhelmed crowd of last week is back today. They're asking themselves, *'Is Lady Lee going to be another Regret?'* Regret, ladies and gentlemen, was the *only* filly ever to win the Kentucky Derby. Today's race then will give us an inkling as to Lady Lee's prospects in the May classic.

"But regardless of her fate, Mr. Robert Smith, owner of Lady Lee, is mighty well pleased with his filly, whom he bought as a yearling for a mere seven hundred dollars. He could not have found a finer investment for his money, and today there's about twenty-five thousand dollars more waiting for her at the finish. A few moments ago in the paddock I asked Mr. Smith what he thought of his filly's chances in today's race. He told me modestly, *'We know she has the speed, but will she go the mile-and-a-sixteenth distance today in the face of such competition as she'll get from Eclipse and Wintertime?'* "

The picture shifted to a husky, powerfully muscled colt, his towering height well in proportion to his great body.

Alec heard Henry say, "That's him!" And the way he said it could mean but one horse, Eclipse.

Yes, Alec admitted to himself, this colt looked the way a Derby winner should look. He had the body and size to carry him a mile and a quarter or farther. And that he had speed had already been proved in his two-year-old victories over shorter distances. Alec's eyes remained focused on Eclipse, and presently he became aware of the similarity between this colt and Satan. Each had the same short thick neck and heavy head, the same muscular body which made every movement at a walk seem so ponderous.

Eclipse's coat was dark brown, so dark it was almost black. Yet in startling contrast he had lots of white on him, with a wide blaze running from forehead to nostrils and long white stockings on all four legs.

Alec listened to the announcer telling of Eclipse's great races as a two-year-old and the high hopes his stable had for him this year. The announcer concluded with, "Back in the paddock Eclipse walked around the place as though he owned it. He showed not one bit of nervousness. His only outward sign of anxiousness was a kick or two while being saddled."

Alec watched the husky colt. Eclipse wasn't showing any sign of nervousness now, either. And he walked as though he owned the track. Well, they'd soon know.

The picture swept down the line of horses, came to a stop, and centered on a close-up of another colt. *Wintertime!* He was a blood bay, solidly built but not too big. He wore a red blinker hood, and Alec noticed that the cup over the right eye was almost completely closed. He turned questioningly to Henry.

The trainer said, "Last year Wintertime had a tendency to run out, sometimes swerving abruptly, almost hurting himself and others. They're trying to correct that with one-eyed blinkers this year, and it seems to be working."

The announcer, too, was telling of the colt's tendency to swerve during the running of a race.

"Wintertime ran straight in last week's race, so maybe his trainer, Don Conover, has licked the colt's bad habit of last year. Don tells me that in addition to the one-eyed blinker hood, he also has a run-out bit on the colt. This bit, ladies and gentlemen, is so designed that when the colt is running straight he has only a smooth plate against the right side of his mouth, but if he pushes out there are sharp prongs that are brought into play which stick him. It sounds cumbersome but it isn't. And if the bit keeps Wintertime in line he should be a colt to reckon with in this race and in those to come.

"Wintertime is strong and game, as he proved in many of his fine races as a two-year-old. Looking at him now you might think he is a small horse, but he isn't. He stands a little over fifteen hands."

Alec turned again to Henry. "He looks like our filly," he said.

"Except for the tail," Henry replied, smiling. "You never saw a prettier tail than he's got."

Alec resumed watching the screen. Wintertime's tail almost touched the ground, and as the colt went into a gallop, the tail flowed like a cloak behind him. The television cameras stayed on him.

"That's Billy Watts up on Wintertime," the announcer was saying. "He's seventeen years old and one of the most promising young riders in the business. He's been with trainer Don Conover for over three years now and has measured up to all the flattering things said and written about him. It's a great tribute to his ability that a trainer like Don Conover has put the youngster up on his stable's top candidate for the Kentucky Derby."

A few minutes later the horses were in the stalls of the

starting gate. Alec's eyes were now on the jockeys, whom he could see behind the wire-mesh doors. He watched Steve Martin trying to soothe Lady Lee as she began acting up. Martin was an old hand. He'd been riding before Alec was born. He was a good rider, competent without being spectacular. He'd get the most out of the filly because he knew everything there was to know about his mounts.

In the number 4 stall, Ted Robinson sat quietly astride Eclipse. Neither he nor the great dark colt with the broad white blaze seemed to be anxious or ready to go. Robinson, still in his early twenties, was one of the great riders of all time, and had been for the past five years. Only the capable Dan Seymour, who had ridden Silver Jet to victory in the Flamingo, was as sought after for his riding services. Consequently Robinson, like Seymour, had his choice of the finest horses in any race. He was a hand-rider, yet polished, too, in the art of knowing when and how to use his whip. To Alec, Eclipse and Ted Robinson were as formidable a combination as Silver Jet and Dan Seymour. Could he and Black Minx compete with them?

But he was getting ahead of himself. There'd be time enough to think about the Derby. He focused his eyes on the outside stall, where Billy Watts sat astride Wintertime. The kid was almost lost behind the colt's red-hooded head. Yet Alec was able to see the paleness of the boy's thin face. He knew how Billy felt, up on a Derby colt, with so much to be gained or lost in this race and the big one to come. The kid was scared but obviously capable in the gate, for he was having no trouble with the colt.

The bell sounded and the gate doors flew open. There was a mad rush of horseflesh and pounding hoofs coming toward the cameras. Heads were pushed out and straining. Above all came the shrill cries of the riders. Alec could only make out Eclipse's white blaze in that great surge.

Then the picture shifted quickly to give a side view of the racing field. Lady Lee was in front by a head, her long legs sweeping the track as her veteran rider, Steve Martin, used his whip in an effort to get clear of the inside horses and move to the rail. Before the first turn he had her out in front by a length. Then he moved over to the rail.

Behind Lady Lee came Eclipse, and Alec saw that there was nothing ponderous about him now, no more so than with Satan when he was in full stride. Ted Robinson, too, was using his whip. But he could not get Eclipse clear of the field and had to take the colt wide as he went around the turn. Alec's eyes left him for the red-hooded Wintertime, who was being bumped by another colt. Alec saw him falter, then pick up stride again. Billy Watts brought him outside and took the turn wide. Alec realized the kid had chosen to waste precious ground rather than chance being bottled up on the rail by older and trickier riders.

Alec watched the leader. Going into the backstretch, Lady Lee had opened two lengths between herself and Eclipse. She was moving easily and under no urging by her rider. Eclipse, too, had settled down and Robinson wasn't asking him for anything more just now. Wintertime came off the turn ahead of the remaining horses, but he was four lengths behind Eclipse and six behind Lady Lee.

"There it is," Alec told Henry. "Our three-horse race!"

Henry only grunted. He was waiting, watching for the move he expected Eclipse to make in the backstretch.

With a half-mile still to go there was a sudden shout from

the stands. Alec's eyes swept from Lady Lee to Eclipse. There was no change, neither was being hustled. But four lengths behind, Billy Watts was urging Wintertime, and the blood bay colt was responding! He stepped up his strides, his long black tail trailing in the rush of wind he was creating.

Alec stood up in his excitement. "Come on!" he yelled. But before the words had left his mouth he saw that it would be a hopeless chase, for Lady Lee and Eclipse had begun moving faster too! Steve Martin was using his heels on the brown filly. Ted Robinson used his whip just once on Eclipse, and then urged the great colt on with hands alone.

The crowd shouted again. The race now was entering its final stage. The horses would extend themselves until they went under the wire. A quarter of a mile still remained.

Wintertime had managed to get two lengths nearer Eclipse by his early bid. But there he stayed, unable to move any closer to the husky brown colt. Lady Lee kept her two-length lead over Eclipse while rounding the back turn and entering the homestretch. Once again, Steve Martin asked his filly for more speed, using his hands and feet and whip. She responded quickly, courageously, her long, thin body stretching out to still greater length.

The screams of the crowd rose to a tumultuous roar, claiming the track and every room in the land where a television set was tuned in to this race. Here in the last furlong of the race was the filly's answer to those who had asked, *"We know she's fast but will she go on?"*

But even as the crowd roared their acclaim at her burst of speed in the stretch, there was movement behind. Eclipse and Wintertime were coming up on her! The shouts became more deafening. Seldom did race fans have the privilege of witnessing such a finish!

Alec and Henry were on their feet, their fists clenched and moving, their voices raised.

Wintertime was still two lengths behind Eclipse but moving with him, stride for stride, neither gaining nor losing ground. Together they narrowed the gap between them and the hard-running Lady Lee until Eclipse had his nose at the filly's saddle, then at her head, *then out front and under the finish wire!*

Alec and Henry sat back in their chairs while Henry's old friend "Red" Dawson, trainer of Eclipse, was being interviewed.

"He's as good a three-year-old as I've ever seen," the bald ex-jockey said. "Sure we'll get some stiff competition from Silver Jet, Golden Vanity, and maybe a few others, but if my colt can carry his speed a mile and a quarter—and I don't see why he can't—they'll have to break records to beat him in the Derby."

Henry wasn't interested in listening to anything his old pal had to say about Eclipse. He had just seen a great filly outrun *but not outgamed.*

# *The Gate*

## 13

During the following week there was no doubt that the Kentucky Derby was close at hand. One couldn't read the newspapers or magazines without being told in glowing terms of "America's greatest sports event in which the noble Kings and Queens of the Turf will race for fame and fortune. Out of this whirlwind mass of thunder and speed will emerge one thoroughbred whose name will be added to the long list of Derby champions which includes the great names of American racing—Exterminator, Zev, Reigh Count, Gallant Fox, Twenty Grand, Cavalcade, Omaha, War Admiral, Whirlaway, Shut Out, Count Fleet, Citation and Assault, to mention only a few."

But Alec didn't need to be reminded that the Derby was less than three weeks away, for Henry began ordering longer and faster works for Black Minx.

"Show me you're a Derby horse and you'll go—only then

will you go!" became Henry's attitude. Not that he said it in so many words. But Alec knew that was what he meant. They had been friends too long for Alec not to know.

There were other things too that gave evidence of how close they were to the Derby. No longer did Henry display the slightest optimism concerning the filly's chances in the approaching classic. And Henry was a man of three distinct moods when it came to training.

In November, when he had brought the filly home, he had said, "I've got a Derby horse, Alec!" That had been mood number one, the mood of lofty optimism. It was understandable because Henry never took any horse unless he was enthusiastic over his prospects of developing a champion.

Since then, months of training had passed. Henry's face had become more settled, more grim, and his remarks more cautious. Number two mood had set in. "I *think* she'll be ready," he'd said.

Now the Derby was upon them, and Henry entered his last mood. He was silent and unsmiling. He *demanded* of the filly and Alec rather than asked. He would send Black Minx up to a mile in her speed works; then he would have her galloped out for another half. And all during the last half mile he would shout to Alec not to let her gallop "so slowly!" Yet he knew as well as Alec how the filly would act as soon as the bit was taken from her. Henry was now the strict taskmaster, more trainer than friend. Yet it made him what he was, as good a man as there was around in getting a horse ready to win the first time out.

Understanding this, Alec ignored Henry's long periods of silence as well as his occasional tirades at the track during a work. He knew that Henry would not permit the filly to be raced in the Kentucky Derby or the Kentucky Oaks *or anywhere else* unless she was ready. Nothing was certain for her or for them at this time.

Nevertheless, Alec continued to keep track of all new developments in the Derby picture. He knew that Wintertime and Lady Lee had left New York to go to Keeneland, Kentucky. They would race there, and then go on to Churchill Downs for Derby Week.

Henry said, "Lady Lee is a narrow-fronted, slab-sided filly but she's *game*. They haven't given her up yet as a Derby horse."

Listening to Henry's terse comment on Lady Lee, Alec wondered if Henry had given up his own filly as a Derby horse. Certainly she displayed no gameness, and could any horse win the classic without it?

After Wintertime and Lady Lee had left New York, another top colt arrived there. Silver Jet was at the track, ready to meet Eclipse in the Wood Memorial Stakes on the following Saturday. It would be the most important preparatory race of all, for those two top colts of the year before would meet for the first time as three-year-olds. Furthermore, each was on his way to the Derby. Silver Jet had been given only light training since his brilliant February victory in the Flamingo, and he was reported to be in his finest shape. Both he and Eclipse would be carrying the same weight of 126 pounds, and the distance would be a mile and a sixteenth. Something just had to give in that race!

Saturday morning, the day of the Wood Memorial and two weeks before the Derby, Henry had Alec take the filly over a mile at top speed. He clocked her, and when she was brought back to him his face was void of emotion.

Alec stroked the filly's sweated neck but his eyes studied Henry. There was no sign of satisfaction in Henry's face, yet disappointment wasn't there either. It had seemed to Alec that Black Minx had really moved along during her mile work. But only the watch would given him any conclusive evidence of her speed, and Henry held it closed tight in his big hand.

"Keep walking her," the trainer directed. But he didn't let them go alone. He walked beside them in silence for a while, then he said, "Alec, don't you think you could do more to make her believe she's running away with you?"

"I'm doing everything I can, Henry." There was a little resentment in Alec's voice as he added, "I keep moving the reins. I keep calling to her to stop."

"Maybe if you got even more excited she'd—"

Alec interrupted, his voice sharp. "I *am* excited, Henry. If you think I'm not—"

"No. No, I'm sorry, Alec." Henry continued walking alongside, then he said, "That last quarter-mile of the Derby is going to be tough. She's got to give more."

"She'll have to give it herself," Alec replied, still angry. "There's only so much we can do."

Nothing more was said. Far up the track was the small mobile starting gate, which Henry had had rolled out from the barn a few days before. As they continued walking toward it, Alec asked, "You're not going to break her from the gate after her work, are you?"

"No, but I want her to stand in the gate to see how she reacts to it. I'll break her from it next week. One or two breaks should be enough. Too much gate work does more harm than good."

The gate was at the end of a chute extension leading from

the track, and as they neared it, Black Minx became uneasy.
Alec felt the quivering of her body and knew that she recognized the gate for what it was. She'd been schooled at the
barrier, he knew, or she wouldn't have raced at all as a two-year-old. He stroked her neck in an attempt to quiet her but
she swerved across the track. He straightened her out, and
Henry took hold of her bridle.

She went forward but her flicking ears gave evidence of
her nervousness. And when Henry had her behind the gate
she began to fight him. She reared, came down, and stood
still, refusing to enter the gate stall.

Alec talked to her, trying to calm her down, but that was
all he could do except, of course, to stick with her. The rest
was up to Henry, the same as it would be in a race, where
there would be an assistant starter to help if she began acting
up at the gate.

Henry's face was grim but his hands and voice were quiet,
gentle but firm. This was not his first experience with a
horse who, for some reason, had an aversion to the gate. He
went slowly, disclosing the patience that had enabled him to
put so many colts under his spell.

"It won't hurt you," he said, making no effort to move
the filly into the stall. He wouldn't get tough with her; it
would only make things more difficult later on.

After a while Alec said, "She's trembling as much as ever."

"I know, but we'll try it again now."

Reluctantly Black Minx took a few steps toward the open
back door of the gate. Henry stopped her before she had a
chance to balk again. He drew her head down to let her sniff
the gate. Her muzzle quivered as it touched the canvas-covered sides of the stall.

Henry moved to the front of her, standing within the stall. After a few moments he coaxed her forward. She took another step under the hand she had learned to obey so well.

Alec leaned forward, close to her neck, offering all the encouragement he could. But he knew his most important job was to be ready for any sudden move the filly might make. If she should unseat him now, there would only be additional problems at the gate. Secure in his saddle, he left the rest up to Henry. He noticed that Black Minx's head was turned toward the door. It was wide open and he wondered that she should be giving it so much attention.

At Henry's bidding she moved again, and this time her forelegs were in the stall before Henry stopped her. Once more the trainer waited, talking softly and stroking her. The front door of the stall was open. What he wanted her to do was to stand in the stall while he clambered about the framework of the gate, fooling with her head, crawling under her and over her, and sliding off her rump—all to make certain she would be accustomed to the hullabaloo that accompanies the start of a race.

Alec felt most of the uneasiness leave the filly while Henry talked to her. She consented to take another few steps and finally stood all the way in her stall.

Henry's face disclosed nothing. He said, "I won't close the doors. Be ready in case she bolts on you." For a few minutes he handled her bridle, and then moved to the side, climbing on the gate's framework, his hands always on her. The filly's eyes followed all his movements.

Alec felt her uneasiness return when Henry leaned against her hindquarters. But she didn't bolt. Henry climbed down and went under her. Like the filly, Alec was conscious of the trainer's every move. He glanced back and saw the abrupt twitches of Black Minx's docked tail. If it had been of normal length it would be lashing about her, he thought, instead of looking like a car's windshield wiper going full speed.

Henry moved behind her, then climbed up on the gate's framework again. Alec saw the pinpoints of light in his eyes, and knew that Henry was satisfied with the progress he'd made so far. It was better than Alec had expected, too. He hadn't thought they'd get the filly into the gate at all. The worst was over.

Then Henry reached for the back door of the stall. He had started to swing it shut when the filly bolted, and Alec could do nothing but let her go. She was halfway down the stretch before she slowed to her easy gallop.

Alec turned her around and brought her back, but Henry had already left the gate. When they reached him, the trainer grumbled, "That's enough. We're through with her for the day."

On the way to the barn Alec said, "You know what it is, don't you, Henry?"

"Sure. She's afraid of the door."

"With good reason—since one was slammed on her tail as a yearling." Alec paused. "Funny that she's never shown any fear of a door in the barn."

"Close quarters in the gate," Henry replied brusquely. "That's it."

"What are you going to do?"

"Not much we can do to make her forget what happened to her tail. That's part of her psychological make-up now."

"You can't race a horse from the gate without closing the doors," Alec said.

"You're not telling me anything." They were nearing the barns before Henry spoke again. "If we find she can't be started in the gate, we'll just have to start her outside it, that's all."

*Outside and behind,* Alec thought but said nothing. The rule read, "The starter may place vicious and unruly horses outside and *behind* the line." With a large Derby field, being placed outside the gate and behind all the other horses would be too much of a handicap for the filly to bear. Yet there was no alternative if she wouldn't start from the gate.

Alec turned in his saddle to look at the short tail which still moved back and forth. There was no doubt in his mind that the filly was well aware of her loss, if not her disfigurement. For in addition to being a thing of beauty, a horse's tail is a necessary appendage. Without one, a horse has no protection against flies and other insects which annoy and hurt her.

As long as Alec could remember, he had loathed the "docked tails" of the hackney ponies in horse shows and the "set tails" of saddle horses. Both practices were cruel, and he had no use for owners who performed them on their horses.

Alec turned and faced forward again. For a few moments he rode in thoughtful silence. Then, "Henry," he began.

"Yes, Alec?"

"There's nothing wrong with the dock of her tail . . . or the root of her tail, if you want to call it that . . . is there?"

"Of course not. See how she moves it about. If she—" Henry stopped, caught hold of the filly's bridle and held her still. "You mean if we gave her a false tail she'd—"

"—have something to fling around," Alec finished for him. "She might even forget all about not having had one for so long. And even if it didn't help quiet her down in the gate, she'd have a switch to keep the flies away from her this summer."

"But it might work in the gate too, Alec," Henry said quickly. "She might forget fast that she ever had an accident."

"Would it be much of a job?"

Henry was already behind the filly, examining her short tail. "No, it wouldn't," he finally replied. "There's enough hair here to be braided with some more."

"Where'll we get the extra hair?"

Henry returned to his former position at the filly's head before answering. "The Black's and Satan's tails are full," he said. "They could use some thinning out. We'll do it tomorrow." He paused to stroke the filly's neck. "I like your suggestion, Alec. It might work. Anyway, it'll do no harm to try. She's a high-headed gal with a complex. Giving her a tail again might make more changes in her than either of us suspects. It just might at that."

They continued toward the barn, Alec sitting thoughtfully in the saddle. It had been quite a morning. Black Minx had worked a fast mile, been introduced to the gate again, and now was going to get a new tail, courtesy of the Black and Satan! Within a few hours' time, too, they'd be watching Eclipse and Silver Jet race in the Wood Memorial Stakes. April 21 was going to be a day to remember!

# The Wood Memorial

## 14

"Good afternoon, ladies and the gentlemen," the announcer said. "We're in the paddock, just prior to the running of New York's last and most important test for Kentucky Derby candidates, the Wood Memorial Stakes at a mile and a sixteenth."

Alec and Henry drew their chairs closer to the television screen as the picture showed the horses and their riders circling the paddock ring. A light, steady drizzle was coming down.

Alec glanced out the window of the attic. There had been an overcast sky all afternoon at Hopeful Farm but it had not rained. "Looks as if they'll be going on a muddy track," he said, turning back to watch the screen.

"Not unless it rains harder and longer than it's doing there now," Henry replied. "The track has too much sand in it ever to get real muddy."

The picture showed a close-up of a gray colt wearing a black blinker hood, and Alec immediately recognized Silver Jet. The colt looked as good as he had when he'd won the Flamingo. His tall, graceful body moved with no evidence of nervousness; his walk was easy and swinging.

Henry said, "The bandages are off in front."

Alec noted the absence of the bandages the colt had worn in the Flamingo. Then he gave his attention to the announcer.

"That's Silver Jet with Danny Seymour up," the man was saying. "This is a formidable combination that has won four races in four starts this past winter in Florida, including the prized Flamingo Stakes. Unraced since March, Silver Jet is out today to jump right back into the thick of the Kentucky Derby picture. And the chances are excellent that he'll do just that. This colt last year was the champion two-year-old, winning almost two hundred thousand dollars for his owner and trainer, Tom Flint of Texas. This year at three, Silver Jet is unbeaten, and he had no trouble traveling over the mile-and-an-eighth distance of the Flamingo. He runs best up front. As you can see, he's wearing blinkers. Silver Jet is inclined to be inquisitive, so the blinkers are put on to keep his eyes to the front and prevent his paying attention to other animals in the race. He's by the great sire Mahmoud and, like most of this sire's colts, has a streak of temperament. As far as Silver Jet is concerned, the temperament is most apt to be displayed in the starting gate. But just now the colt is as calm as the best mannered of stable ponies."

Silver Jet's small head was being given plenty of free rein by Dan Seymour, yet he walked slowly, completely at ease, and with an air of confidence. His long gray mane and tail hung still in the drizzling rain.

Alec watched Seymour sitting quietly in the saddle, his small, shriveled face disclosing as little interest in the paddock activities as his mount. But all that would change once they went to the post.

". . . Silver Jet was the winter favorite to win the Kentucky Derby," the announcer was saying.

Henry grunted. "A tactless place to mention this," he said, "but the Derby has never been won by a *gray*."

Alec's eyes didn't leave the screen. *No,* he thought, *but there's always a first time, and Silver Jet could do it.* He saw a tall man wearing a large, flowing raincoat walk across the paddock to Silver Jet.

"That's Tom Flint," Henry said. "He sat next to me at the sales when I bought the filly."

Flint was talking to his jockey. He had his wide-brimmed hat pulled low on his head; it was as good as an umbrella in keeping the rain from him.

The announcer said, "I asked Tom Flint a few moments ago how he felt about Silver Jet's first big eastern prep for the Derby. His answer was, *'Silver Jet is ready, but were you ever scared?'* That's all he said, ladies and gentlemen, but Tom Flint is no different from a good many other owners of Derby candidates at this time. They're all a little scared, for anything can happen now and in the coming Derby."

The picture shifted to the husky brown colt with the white face. The announcer continued, "Here's a good reason for Tom Flint's being scared today. It's Eclipse, second-rated two-year-old last year and winner of Saturday's Experimental Number Two in the sizzling time of one minute and forty-four seconds for the mile and a sixteenth. Today's race is over the same distance and all colts will be carrying equal weight of one hundred twenty-six pounds which, incidentally, is the weight they'll carry in the Kentucky Derby. That's the young veteran Ted Robinson up on Eclipse. He's the colt's regular rider."

Ted Robinson sat easily on the big, muscular colt. The jockey displayed the confidence of Silver Jet's rider, and the husky colt beneath him was equally calm. When Eclipse walked, he carried his big head higher than had the gray colt, and while his white-stockinged legs moved with none of Silver Jet's easy grace, the assurance of speed was there.

Beside them trotted a short, stocky man carrying an umbrella over his head.

"That's Eclipse's trainer, 'Red' Dawson, talking to Robinson," the announcer said.

Alec glanced away from the screen. Dawson was an old friend of Henry's. "I'll bet he's scared too," he said.

Henry grunted. "He's been around too long to be scared. He was riding horses before Tom Flint made his first hundred dollars."

Alec smiled. "He sure looks funny carrying that big umbrella."

"He's fussy about gettin' his head wet. He doesn't have thick red hair any more. Under that hat it's as bare as a billiard ball."

The television cameras left Eclipse and followed the other horses about the paddock oval.

"Nine colts will be going to the post, ladies and gentlemen, and all of them are Derby eligibles," the announcer said. "It must be evident by this time to the owners and trainers of these other Derby hopefuls that Eclipse rules the eastern roost and only Silver Jet can unseat him today. But hope runs high at this time of year, and there's always a possibility of an upset in today's race. Yet these other colts, most of them beaten by Eclipse last Saturday, will be anchored today with one hundred twenty-six pounds. Unless they show something altogether unexpected it would seem hopeless to start them in the Derby on May fifth. It is reported that Eclipse and Silver Jet will be shipped to Churchill Downs on Monday, providing they cool out well after today's race."

A bugle sounded, calling the horses to the post. In single file they left the paddock and paraded on the track. The announcer was giving the names and racing backgrounds of the colts who would race against Eclipse and Silver Jet. The only one that aroused Alec's interest was the small bay Moonstruck, who had run second to Golden Vanity in the Santa Anita Derby in February.

The rain came down harder as the colts neared the starting gate, and the majority of people standing in front of the grandstand scuttled under the stands. All the horses went behind the gate, turned, and entered their stalls. Just then the rain slackened to a light drizzle again, and the crowd rushed out from beneath the protective stands to watch the race. The gate doors closed. The break would come any second.

Alec asked, "How are Eclipse and Silver Jet in the mud?"

"It's not muddy," Henry insisted. "The track's good even if it is a little slippery." He paused. "But to answer your question, I hear the two of 'em can take mud or leave it alone. It won't make any difference to them if there's a muddy track in the Derby."

The bell sounded and the gate doors were opened. Moonstruck broke fast on the inside as Alec had guessed he would.

But from his outside post position Silver Jet was away just as fast; he came racing toward the cameras, his hooded head stretched out.

Alec's eyes quickly shifted to the center of the field, trying to find Eclipse's white face. He found it in time to see the big colt stumble coming out of the gate. Eclipse picked up stride again, but not before the horses on either side of him had closed in front of him. Alec saw Ted Robinson pull up the big colt.

Moonstruck came flying into the front of the television cameras and the picture quickly shifted to show a side view of the field as the colts thundered past, racing for the first turn. Running on the rail, Moonstruck pulled clear of the field. Far on the outside Silver Jet pulled clear too but Moonstruck, having less distance to travel, outran the gray colt to the turn. Dan Seymour took Silver Jet just to the right of the bay leader.

Behind them came the closely packed field with Eclipse in fifth position, still blocked from settling into his great strides.

Watching the horses race around the turn, Henry shook his head. "Eclipse is licked," he grunted. "He'll never get out of there in time."

The leaders came off the turn, and Alec had to admit that the race looked hopeless for the big colt. Already there were five lengths between the two leaders and the rest of the field. And now Seymour began using his whip on Silver Jet. He struck the gray colt just once, and Silver Jet surged past Moonstruck to take the lead. Then Seymour put aside his whip, riding easily and saving his mount.

Behind them, the third horse leading the rest of the field

pulled a length clear, going after Moonstruck. And suddenly out of the pack and still on the inside came Eclipse's white face.

Alec let out a shout. "Here he comes, Henry!"

Eclipse was in full chase now. He had settled into stride and Ted Robinson let him go without using his whip. Ahead of them was the third horse by two lengths, a length beyond him was Moonstruck, and another length beyond was Silver Jet. The pace was fast but Eclipse was clear of the tightly packed field behind him. Now he had a chance in his chase of the flying gray colt!

Halfway down the backstretch Ted Robinson used his whip and Eclipse was in a drive. He closed the distance between him and the horse ahead, who was now racing at Moonstruck's flanks.

Alec watched closely as they all went into the far turn with Silver Jet still a good two lengths in front of Moonstruck. He saw Moonstruck begin to wobble and knew the sprinter was through. The colt just behind him was ready to give up too. Now, if Eclipse could get past them, he might have a chance of catching Silver Jet in the homestretch.

Moonstruck was wobbling so much he was bearing out going around the turn, taking with him the colt behind, who was as spent as he was.

Henry leaped to his feet. "Inside, Robinson! *Go inside of them on the rail!*"

Alec too was up from his chair. Even before he saw Ted Robinson go for his whip again, he knew the veteran jockey would take advantage of the opening on the rail. Eclipse responded quickly and pressed inside the two tired colts in front of him. Yet even as he made his bid, the two colts came to an abrupt stop. Moonstruck wobbled against Eclipse and crowded him against the rail.

Robinson pulled up Eclipse, bounced off the rail, and then slammed back against Moonstruck. Neither horse went down, and in a fraction of a second Eclipse was again in the clear. He seemed unhurt and was full of run but Robinson made no effort to catch Silver Jet. A horse could take just so many bad breaks during the running of a race, and Eclipse had had more than his share. The veteran jockey let the colt go but wisely did not urge him, as far ahead Silver Jet neared the finish line.

Alec and Henry watched the gray colt being driven all out down the homestretch by Dan Seymour. And the jockey did not slow him down after passing beneath the finish wire. Silver Jet went a full mile and a quarter before being brought down to an easy gallop.

Henry said, "Seymour had orders to work him the Derby distance. I wonder if they'll announce the time for it."

The television cameras stayed on Silver Jet until he was jogging back. Then they picked up Eclipse and the announcer said, "I don't believe he hurt himself in that unfortunate jam on the turn, and Moonstruck looks all right too. It was just one of those bad breaks that come all too often in racing."

Henry's eyes didn't leave Eclipse all the time the husky colt appeared on the screen. "He never had a chance today, never had room to do his running. This race has nothing to do with the Derby picture."

Alec smiled. "You'd better be careful what you say, Henry."

"Why?"

"I think I just heard someone give Silver Jet's time for the mile and a sixteenth. It was a minute and forty-three seconds."

Henry turned to Alec, his eyes showing his great surprise. "If you heard right," he said, "I'm wrong, Alec."

Silver Jet was in the winner's circle, and the announcer said, "The time for the mile and a sixteenth, ladies and gentlemen, was one minute and forty-three seconds, *which equals the race record!*"

"You were right, Alec," Henry said. "And he did it on a wet track, too! It's hard to believe that he went a second faster than Eclipse did last Saturday in beating Lady Lee."

Now Tom Flint was standing beside his colt, and the crowd closed in upon the ring while photographers took pictures. When they had finished, Dan Seymour dismounted and Silver Jet was led from the ring.

The announcer looked up at Tom Flint's towering frame during the interview and asked, "You had your colt go the full Derby distance, Mr. Flint. Would you tell us his time?"

Flint's big face showed nothing, but his eyes were very bright. "Since a lot of watches were probably on him, I don't mind telling you," he said in his deep voice. "He worked the Derby distance in two minutes, four and a fifth seconds."

"That's fast enough to have won most of the past Derbies," the announcer said.

"Most of 'em," Flint repeated evasively.

"You mustn't be as scared now as you were in the paddock before the race, Mr. Flint."

Silver Jet's owner and trainer buttoned the top of his raincoat. "I'm still scared," he said.

"Of Golden Vanity?" the announcer asked.

Flint took a step away from the television camera, then stopped. "Of Golden Vanity, Eclipse, Wintertime, Lady Lee, and just about any and *all* of the colts we'll be up against in the Derby." He shoved his hands into his pockets and left the ring with Dan Seymour.

The announcer was about to conclude the program when a note was handed to him. After reading it, he said, "Eclipse has been examined and found to be unhurt. He'll be shipped to Churchill Downs on Monday as planned."

Alec turned off the television set. "Are *we* going to Churchill Downs next week as planned, Henry?" he asked.

"After today's race a lot of people will be saying that Silver Jet is going to be the colt Golden Vanity will have to beat in the Derby," Henry said. "Perhaps so. Anyway, they're the same type of front runner. It should be a good show going down that last furlong."

Alec turned away from him, thinking that once again Henry had evaded a direct answer to his question.

But Henry hadn't finished. "We couldn't miss such a show, could we, Alec? *Yes, we'll be going to Churchill Downs next week.*"

When they left the attic Alec knew they'd be taking the filly to Kentucky, but he was certain of nothing else. Henry hadn't said if she'd run in the Derby or the Oaks or in any one of a number of shorter and less important races. But it was enough to know they were going. And he felt that Henry wouldn't be going to Churchill Downs unless Black Minx was ready to race.

# "Show Those Hardboots!"

## 15

It rained hard the next day but Alec and Henry had plenty of inside work to do. Together they groomed the Black, Alec working on the stallion's sweeping tail. He always kept it clean and free from tangles. Occasionally, as he did today, he thinned it out. First he brushed and combed the heavy tail, which reached almost to the stall floor, then carefully he selected a few strands at a time and pulled them out. He knew that the root or dock of the tail was not sensitive and that no horse would object to a thinning out, provided too many hairs were not pulled at the same time.

The Black pushed his slender muzzle toward Alec's chest. Fondly, tenderly, Alec stroked his horse. The stallion stood quietly beneath his touch. The few extra pounds the Black had been carrying at the beginning of the breeding season were gone. He was now lean and hard, almost in racing trim.

Even more than the Black's physical well-being, Alec was

impressed by the stallion's remarkable adjustment to life at Hopeful Farm. No longer was he as nervous and excitable as he had been in the early days, and he seemed to understand his freedom in pastures and paddocks. One day Alec had even caught him standing at his stall window, neighing at Satan in the front paddock, much as a couple of good neighbors might have done.

After Alec had thinned out the stallion's tail as much as he wanted, he went to Henry. "We'll need plenty more for the filly," he said.

Henry answered impatiently, "Come on, Alec. We'll get some more hair from Satan, and if that's not enough we'll have Napoleon contribute some."

During the next hour they went from Satan to Napoleon. Then, still needing more hair, they went to the mares, thinning out one tail after another. When they had enough, they started for Black Minx's stall.

Henry grinned as he opened the door. "Looks kinda pretty, doesn't it?"

Alec nodded. The false tail was predominately black from the stallions and the bay mares, but intermingled with it were plenty of Napoleon's long gray hairs. "Like a darkheaded man getting prematurely gray," he said.

The filly turned to them, her bright eyes disclosing her eagerness to leave the stall. Henry said, "Not now, girl. Later we'll go out for a walk but not just now. Alec, you get at her head and hand me a little of the hair at a time as I ask for it." He took a few long strands, then handed the rest of the hair to Alec.

For a long while, Alec held Black Minx's halter and watched Henry braid the hair to the filly's own, using a heavy, strong sewing thread. Little by little Black Minx was acquiring a new tail!

She was aware something was going on. Yet she remained in the corner of her stall without kicking. Alec handed Henry more strands of hair as they were called for and kept talking to the filly, assuring her she'd like the results of what they were doing.

It was a good hour before Henry finished and stepped back from the filly, examining his job. Finally he turned to Alec and said, "That's it, and it's not a bad job if I do say so myself. Not bad at all."

Alec smiled and nodded in agreement. Already the filly was swishing her new tail, and her eyes grew brighter in her excitement at the unfamiliar sound of it striking against the side of her stall. She swished harder, bringing the tail across her hind legs and finally swinging it all the way around to her flanks and back. Alec left her head to stand outside the stall with Henry.

Black Minx moved quickly to the center of her stall, then stopped. She seemed content just to stand still and swish her tail. Her eyes lost none of their brightness and her small ears were pitched forward. Occasionally she tossed her head, snorting, but for the most part her tail did all the moving.

"She missed having a tail, all right," Alec said.

"She sure did, and it makes her appearance a lot neater. I'd forgotten how much I missed it, too."

The end of the false tail came just above the filly's hocks. It could have been a little longer, a little fuller, but, nevertheless, it was a remarkable improvement.

Alec said, "Napoleon's hairs sure look strange amid all that black."

Henry laughed. "Something old from Nap, something new from the others," he said. "Maybe it'll bring us luck."

"I hope so," Alec replied.

A little later they left Black Minx alone, giving her a chance to become thoroughly familiar with her new tail.

It continued raining all that afternoon, through the night, and all the next morning. But early Monday afternoon it stopped and Henry hurriedly saddled the filly. He was afraid that more rain might keep her in her stall another day. She needed a long gallop, but he didn't want her going out in the rain for fear she'd catch cold and upset all his plans for the trip to Churchill Downs on Thursday.

Alec arrived at the barn at the appointed time for Black Minx's workout, and Henry boosted him up. He turned in his saddle and noted that the filly wasn't swishing her tail as much as she had done the day before. Maybe, he decided, she had become used to it already, had accepted it, and had forgotten that only two days before she'd had none.

"She seems to be taking her new tail for granted now," he called to Henry as the filly was led up the road.

"I like to think so," Henry said. "That's what we were hoping she'd do."

Alec nodded. *Yes,* he thought, *that's exactly what we want. If she forgets that she has been without a tail, she'll forget the accident that caused it to be amputated. Then she won't be so apt to get excited in the close quarters of the gate.*

A few moments later they were on the rain-sodden track, and Henry said, "Just let her gallop two miles, Alec. When you're finished we'll try having her stand at the gate again."

Nodding, Alec let her go. She moved into her slow gallop,

her feet stepping lightly over the mud. Alec soon learned that for all the good the new tail did for her appearance, and for all it might do to help matters at the gate, it certainly did not lend her any added incentive to run. She moved no faster and no slower than before.

Several times during the first mile he felt her grab for the bit, but he kept it away from her. She continued her slow gallop, although he constantly urged her to hasten her strides. Only by taking hold of the bit would she run for him. She still had a mind of her own, and was going to have her own way under saddle.

At the end of the two-mile gallop he took her back to Henry at the starting gate. When she saw it her ears pricked forward, but other than that there was no indication of interest or fear.

Just behind the gate, Henry reached for her bridle and led her toward one of the starting stalls. She walked with him, never balking, and Henry was grinning when he had her standing in the stall.

He stroked the filly's head, and said to Alec, "The new tail is working. I could close the doors today but I'm not going to do it. It'll be enough just to have her stand here for a few minutes."

Alec continued to sit quietly in the saddle. There was nothing else for him to do, except to wonder at the swiftness with which Black Minx had accepted her new tail and had forgotten being without one and the reason for it.

A few moments later they were on their way back to the barn. It had been a most quiet hour but Alec was glad of it. Starting Thursday morning and continuing through the following week, he would have little free time. He knew there would be many days at Churchill Downs when he would look back with longing upon the quiet hours spent here at the farm.

The next day Alec became conscious of an increasing feeling of tension. His excitement mounted until he couldn't sit still, and when he had no immediate jobs he created something to do.

He knew Silver Jet and Eclipse had arrived at Churchill Downs. He also knew that Golden Vanity, Wintertime, and Lady Lee were at the Keeneland track about fifty miles from Churchill Downs; they would race in the Blue Grass Stakes at that track on Thursday. That was the day on which he and Henry and the filly would leave Hopeful Farm for Kentucky.

Meanwhile, Alec studied every item about the three-year-olds that appeared in the newspapers. One of these gave an account of Golden Vanity's latest work at the Keeneland track, and Alec read it with avid interest.

Golden Vanity, favored by many to win the Kentucky Derby at Churchill Downs a week from Saturday, breezed seven-eighths of a mile in 1:29 at the Keeneland oval today. Nino Nella, his regular rider, was up.

Without question Golden Vanity is the best three-year-old to be bred in California. His owner, Mr. Lionel Graham, is bringing along his own cheering section to the Derby.

The chestnut colt has worked impressively since his arrival from California two weeks ago. However, the consensus among the observers at Keeneland is this: "We want to see what Golden Vanity does when some other horse looks him in the eye. He had pretty much his own way on the West Coast but things will be different here in the East. There's many a fast horse that falls short of expectations when another runner races him head on head. Golden Vanity has speed. We know that. But so have Lady Lee and Wintertime, and they'll both be in there against him in the Blue Grass Stakes on Thursday. We'll know more then about Golden Vanity's Derby status."

Lady Lee and Wintertime, who ran second and third respectively to Eclipse in Experimental Number Two, arrived at Keeneland last week, and are ready to go in the Blue Grass Stakes.

Alec showed this story to Henry. After reading it the trainer said, "That's the way I feel about Golden Vanity too. Wait until something looks him in the eye."

Wednesday was busier than any other day, for early the following morning they'd be on the road, bound for Churchill Downs. Alec was thankful for everything that kept his hands and mind occupied. He had less time then to think of the Kentucky Derby.

In the morning he broke Black Minx from the gate. They had had very little trouble closing the doors on her. After he gave her the bit for seven-eighths of a mile, as Henry ordered, he galloped out a full mile and a half. As usual Henry said nothing about the filly's clocking, and there was nothing in his face to show whether it had been good time or bad. Henry's only remark was, "Well, that's the last one for this track. I'll cool her out now."

During the afternoon and evening Alec had to do a countless number of jobs. For the last time he examined all the mares, foals, and stallions; he went over everything again with his father, who would be in charge during his absence, and made certain there were no misunderstandings between them. He drove himself ruthlessly every minute and felt better for it.

Before going to bed he helped pack the tack trunks and put them into the van. He bedded down the van's stalls for the filly and Napoleon. Henry had decided he wanted Napoleon along. He had announced that the old gray would provide companionship for Black Minx; but Alec knew that Napoleon was being taken along more as a companion for Henry than for the filly. Napoleon had been stabled with Satan and the Black during their racing days. Now it was only right, as Henry saw it, that the old gelding should go to the track with them on this new venture.

After breakfast the next morning, they loaded the filly and Napoleon into the van. The first streaks of light were showing in the sky when Henry climbed behind the wheel. Alec went to the back of the van, where he'd stay with the horses until they arrived safely at Churchill Downs. It would be a long drive—more than twenty-four hours—with stops along the way to rest and walk the horses.

As Henry started the van, Alec again called good-by to his mother and father, who stood with the three hired men. His mother, so small and plump, yet so delicate in appearance, waved back and called after him, "Son, hold on to those reins and let that filly run. Show those hardboots!"

Alec smiled at his mother's words. Only a short time ago she didn't know what a "filly" was, much less that "hardboots" was a group name for Kentucky horsemen. As the van went down the driveway he turned to the stallion barn. "Here we go, Black," he said. "Here *you* go again!"

The van turned onto the country road, and Alec remained at the side door until he could no longer see the rolling pastures and white fences of Hopeful Farm.

Late in the afternoon, they stopped at a gasoline station on the Pennsylvania Turnpike, and there they heard the radio announcement of the results of the Blue Grass Stakes at Keeneland, Kentucky.

"Golden Vanity gave one of the greatest exhibitions of speed ever seen on a Kentucky track in defeating Wintertime and Lady Lee in new race record time of one minute forty-eight and three-fifths seconds for the mile and eighth. He swept under the wire three lengths in front of Wintertime and seven lengths ahead of Lady Lee. To lend added emphasis as *the horse to beat* in the Kentucky Derby, Golden Vanity's head was pulled sideways by Nino Nella during the last eighth of a mile in the jockey's efforts to slow down his mount. The California-bred colt is now the red-hot favorite to win. . . ."

Henry took Alec's arm. "C'mon, we've heard all we need to. Let's get goin'."

Alec said, "It looks as if you and those Keeneland people will have to change your tune now about Golden Vanity."

"Maybe so," the trainer said, climbing into the van's cab. "He'll be out in front for the first mile, that's a cinch." Henry disappeared inside the cab. As Alec climbed through the side door, he heard Henry add, "Like I said before, it's going to be a good show, all right."

Alec sat down in his canvas chair, looking at Black Minx. *It sure is,* he thought, *and I wonder if we're going to be in it!*

# *Churchill Downs*

## 16

Early the next morning, Alec and Henry were in southern Ohio. Behind them lay the mountainous mining country of Pennsylvania and West Virginia. No longer did the road twist and squirm its way past slag dumps, coal fields, and gigantic mills with chimneys belching red-black smoke into the sky. Now in the gray light of dawn the road was level and straight, passing through the rich and newly plowed farmlands of the Ohio Valley.

They did not stop until they had crossed the Ohio River into Kentucky, and then they paused only long enough to eat and to care for the filly and Napoleon. Henry was anxious to reach Churchill Downs by early afternoon.

In northern Kentucky the land once more became almost mountainous, and then, as they drove on, gently rolling. Soon farms appeared along the road, but the fields were mostly unplowed, showing little spring planting. Instead

acre after acre was in pasture, and the number of horses grazing in these fields grew as Alec and Henry neared the heart
of the bluegrass country.

Finally they had to stop for gas. As Alec slipped down
from the back of the van Henry said, "Just a few more hours
now. How are they riding?"

"They're all right. How about you?"

"I'm in good shape," Henry replied. "The naps I got last
night are holding me up okay. Are you going to get through
the rest of the day all right?"

"Sure," Alec said. "There's nothing wrong with a straw
bed. The horses and I had more rest than you did."

They bought a morning newspaper at the gasoline station,
and then started on their way once more. Alec moved the
filly over and stood beside her as he talked to Henry through
the small barred window between the cab and the back of
the van. He held the newspaper.

"Did you see this story on Golden Vanity's win yesterday?" he asked.

"Just the headline. It's pretty much what we heard yesterday on the radio."

"But the way he did it, Henry."

"What about it?"

"Lady Lee got out ahead of him and led around the first
turn," Alec told his friend. "Then Nino Nella gave Golden
Vanity the signal and the colt bore down, passing her and
having his own way to the finish."

"I still don't get what you mean," Henry said, without
taking his eyes off the road.

"Well, it looks as though Lady Lee looked him in the eye,
and you said—"

Henry interrupted. "We didn't mean in the early part of the race. Wait until it happens at the head of the homestretch."

"If it does," Alec said, "it's going to take something awfully fast to get up there with him."

"Yeah, I know."

They were traveling down the road from Paris to Lexington, the "Avenue of the Thoroughbred." For miles on either side of them were endless wooden fences, some painted white, others brown and black with creosote. Still others were made of stone. All of them protected the thoroughbreds who grazed within the rolling pastures.

Henry said, "Don't scratch Wintertime off your list of topnotch Derby horses just because he got beat again yesterday."

"I'm not. But here's a story that says Lady Lee is out of the Derby."

"Yeah, I saw that."

"Her owner says that he had to use good common sense in deciding to withdraw her from the Derby," Alec told Henry. "He will concentrate on filly races instead. He had given her a couple of throws at the colts, but her defeats by Eclipse in Experimental Number Two and by Golden Vanity and Wintertime yesterday at Keeneland prove to him that the Derby is out of her reach. He claims she's too fine a filly to be broken up trying to lick the colts. She'll run in the Kentucky Oaks instead of in the Derby."

"He's right, of course, but it's too bad," Henry said.

"Why? You mean you wanted to see her go into the Derby?"

Henry's big shoulders moved beneath his jacket. "Then

she wouldn't have been in the Oaks," he said.

Alec didn't bother to ask Henry for an explanation of what he meant. He could guess. He realized that Henry was still trying to make up his mind whether it should be the Derby or the Oaks for their filly. And if Black Minx went into the Oaks she wouldn't have things her own way, as she might have had without Lady Lee in it.

He put the newspaper aside, his hand thoughtfully stroking the filly's back. She swished her new tail at him but otherwise remained quiet. He checked her shipping bandages to make certain they were secure, then resumed looking out the window. He didn't talk to Henry while they drove through the light traffic in Lexington.

Soon they were on the outskirts of town, passing the Keeneland racetrack. The race meeting there had ended the day before, and many horse vans were rolling out of the beautiful park. Some, like their own, were carrying Derby hopefuls to Churchill Downs.

"Henry?"

"Yes, Alec?" Henry turned his head slightly. His face was bristling with more than a day's growth of stiff gray hair.

"The Oaks is only a mile and a sixteenth. We know she could travel that at a good clip. Maybe she'd beat Lady Lee. There aren't any other fillies in the race to worry about."

Henry pushed back his worn hat. "I know all that, Alec." He thrust out his square jaw. "But there's only one Derby."

Alec's mouth got a little tight. "Yes, there's only one," he said quietly. "But it's become a *sprint* of a full mile and a quarter. It requires not only speed but stamina and courage. If you ask me, that's too much to ask of a colt so early in his three-year-old year, let alone a filly."

Henry said nothing. His bowlegs swung a little as he lifted a foot from the accelerator, slowing down so as not to get too close to a horse van directly ahead of him. He regained speed before speaking again.

"A lot of horsemen like to accept the challenge the Derby offers us and our three-year-olds. We know how hard it is to get a young horse in hand to meet the exacting conditions of the Derby. We do it, or try to do it because, like I say, it's a challenge . . . and if we lick it our horse usually goes on to still greater heights."

Alec's mouth had tightened again. "You're getting away from what I meant, Henry. I was talking about fillies in the Derby . . . and there's only been one who went to the winner's circle. That was Regret, in 1915."

"I wouldn't have brought Black Minx along if I didn't think she had a chance," Henry returned quietly.

For another hour they rode, moving ever closer to Louisville and Churchill Downs. The *feel* of the Derby became stronger. It was in the air all about them. It came from pastures and barns, from the roaring wheels of other vans before and behind their own. It came from the eyes and voices of people lining the streets of small towns between Keeneland and Louisville.

On the outskirts of Louisville, Alec moved from his chair to the cab window again. "I've been wondering if there have ever been any Derby winners who made their first start of the year in the Derby," he said.

Henry didn't answer immediately, and Alec knew his friend was either thinking about the question put to him or wasn't going to bother to reply. Perhaps Henry was fed up with his questions, but Alec was determined not to stop asking them. Not until the Derby was over.

Finally Henry said, "Way back in the teens and twenties three horses won the Derby the first time out, if I remember correctly. Exterminator did it in 1918, Sir Barton the following year, and then Morvich in 1922."

"But none since then?"

"No," Henry grunted. "Aren't they enough?"

"Maybe it's harder to do it these days."

"Maybe." Henry's face lightened in a grin, his first grin in many miles. "I'm old enough to think it can still be done!" He paused while slowing down for a traffic light. "But if it'll make you feel easier I'll tell you that Jet Pilot won the Derby in 1947 with just a six-furlong race before the classic."

"Will you give the filly a race before the Derby?"

"Maybe," Henry said, starting up the van once more with the change of lights.

Going through Louisville, Henry took as many back streets as possible. But there was no way for him or the drivers of other vans to avoid the heavy traffic, for Churchill Downs was only ten minutes from the heart of the city. When the famous racecourse had been opened for the first Kentucky Derby in 1875 it was outside the city limits. Now the corporate limits of Louisville extended far beyond Churchill Downs.

All the way to the track the huge horse vans were given the courtesy of the road by city drivers, who were accustomed to the lumbering trucks moving cautiously through their crowded streets at this time of year. Many a resident driver looked out his car window, calling loudly, "You got a Derby colt in there?" And if he got an affirmative answer from a van's cab, his eyes lighted. "Which one, Boss?"

Alec remained silent during the drive through the city. He sat in his chair, his eyes leaving the moving cars only to look at the black filly. Pressure and tension were mounting within him. And he knew there wouldn't be any let-up during the days to come. Instead it would get worse. He tried to think of the calmness and tranquility of Hopeful Farm. But it didn't help. It seemed that Hopeful Farm had never existed. He was being swept into the all-engulfing whirlpool of the Kentucky Derby, and there was nothing he could do about it.

Within a short time he saw the grandstand spires of Churchill Downs, reaching high above the homes adjacent to the race course. Then Henry was driving the van beside a wire fence and finally turning into the entrance to the stable area. Ahead of them were long sheds and barns, horses and vans, trainers and owners. Beyond was the brown ribbon of the track over which the great race had been run for more than three-quarters of a century. And still farther beyond loomed the gigantic grandstand, clubhouse, and bleachers where more than a hundred thousand people would watch the Kentucky Derby, just one week from the following day.

This was Churchill Downs.

Henry stopped the van in line behind others. Pulling on the handbrake, he left the cab. "I'll register at the Secretary's office," he told Alec. "Stick inside."

*As if I'd leave the filly now,* Alec thought. He went to her, knowing that he wanted companionship more than she did. He was still with her when Henry returned a short while later.

The trainer looked through the small window. "All okay back there?"

Alec nodded and the van moved on again slowly, passing horses being unloaded, horses being walked by stable boys. The smell of wood smoke from small fires was strong in the air. Bandages, cloths, coolers, and the countless items that make up a horse's laundry were hanging on lines. Over the loud voices of people and even above the roar of motors came the shrill neighs and nickering of horses. Alec had been at Hopeful Farm so long he had forgotten the commotion, the excitement of a track. And this was no ordinary race meeting that would begin tomorrow afternoon. This was the setting for the swiftly approaching Derby!

"Henry, which colts are here?" he asked.

"Eclipse and Silver Jet are the big ones. There are a couple other Derby horses who'll go only if it's a muddy track. That's all the information I had time to get in the Secretary's office, except that Golden Vanity and Wintertime are now on their way over from Keeneland. We beat them in." He smiled. "That's one race we've won, anyway."

"How many horses do they expect to start in the Derby?"

"There's no way of telling how many will be shipped in," Henry said. "They were surprised to see me here. Maybe more trainers will surprise 'em next week."

Alec thought again of the long list of three-year-olds nominated for the Kentucky Derby last February. There had been more than a hundred. A great number of them had been hopelessly beaten in preparatory races, yet he knew their owners might nevertheless start them in the Derby. And would there be others, too, colts and fillies like Black Minx, unraced and untried? Next week they would know.

At the end of the stable area Henry brought the van to a stop before Barn 10. When he appeared at the side door, Alec pushed the gangway down to him and checked the floor matting to make certain it would not slip.

Henry said, "All the Derby horses will be at this end of the stable area. Eclipse and Silver Jet are just up from us in Barn Eleven."

They unloaded Napoleon first. Then the filly was taken down the gangway. They had no trouble with her, for the sight of grass after her long trip made her more than eager to leave the van.

"Take her for a short sightseeing tour while I fix up Napoleon and get her stall ready," Henry said.

The early afternoon was more balmy than hot. Black Minx pulled toward the grass on the other side of the stable runway, and Alec went along with her. He let her graze a few moments, then pulled her up. "C'mon, girl," he said, "we need to get the travel kinks out of our legs."

At his touch she moved beside him, walking a little sideways and fighting her lead shank. She neighed constantly and shook her small head. But Alec was not disturbed by her restless antics. She had been on the road a long time.

Beneath the overhang of their barn, he saw Henry talking to three men with pencils and pads in their hands. Knowing they were reporters, he kept Black Minx away. But they turned searching eyes on him and at the filly as he led her down the runway.

This was Derby Town, the backstage of racing. The cluttered activity of unloading vans, of jockeys, exercise boys, owners, trainers, grooms, and the multitude of people directly or indirectly concerned with racehorses milled about the stable area. It didn't make things easier for him or the filly. But there was no escape, for they were now a part of Derby Town.

Only on the track was it quiet, for it was long past the

hours of gallops and breezes and works. Alec led the filly toward it, seeking a few moments' reprieve from the clamor of barns and runways.

Barn 11 was just off the road to his left. He saw the crowd standing in front of the stall nearest him. The area in front of the door was roped off, preventing people from getting too close to the horse whose head was over his half-door. Alec had no trouble recognizing Silver Jet's small gray head. Standing near the colt was the towering Tom Flint, wearing the same wide-brimmed sombrero he'd worn when Alec had seen him on television. But this was not a picture on a screen; this was real.

Tom Flint was talking to newsmen, but he stopped to glance at the filly as she walked past. The eyes of reporters, grooms, and all the others were on her for a moment before they turned back again to Silver Jet. Alec heard Flint tell the newsmen, "If we have a fast track for the Derby I won't be too worried about the result."

Alec left the gray colt behind, going carefully around a parked van and milling people, all eying the filly and some asking, "That a Derby horse, son?" His standard reply was, "We don't know yet."

At the far end of Barn 11, another group stood in front of a similarly roped-off stall. Alec saw Eclipse's white face and big head. Holding the colt's halter was a man as short and heavy as Henry. He wore no hat and his bald head was bared to the sun. Alec recognized "Red" Dawson, trainer of Eclipse. He heard Dawson tell the reporters, "Our colt is sharp and getting sharper every day now. If we don't get any bad breaks like we did in the Wood Memorial, we'll catch Silver Jet in the big one."

Alec led the filly on, saying over and over to himself, "This is all real. We're part of the show." He wasn't scared but he couldn't get into the spirit of things. After his months spent at Hopeful Farm, he found the pressure of the Derby a most difficult way of going back to the races. Yet within him surged a rhythmic beat of what he knew was stimulation. One could not be a part of the Derby picture without feeling all the tradition and prestige behind it.

He put his hand on Black Minx's neck and she jumped at his touch. He was aware then that she was as keyed up as he was.

The gate to the track was open but he led the filly away from it and walked along the high wire fence separating the track from the stable area. But here too were signs which told of the imminence of the approaching Derby. Around the mile track sped tractors, harrowing and watering the surface to get it into the finest possible condition for the classic race.

Alec's gaze ranged over the great stands beyond, their multitude of seats empty and waiting. Starting the next day, they would fill a little more with each afternoon's racing, until on the following Saturday they would overflow into bleachers and infield, onto the track and countless rooftops.

Alec turned around at the noise of an approaching van. Barn 8 was nearest to him, and the van stopped before it. Hundreds of people were emerging from the stable area and hurrying toward the barn. Alec knew of only one colt who could attract so much attention upon his arrival. Before the crowd reached the van, the gangway was down and Golden Vanity had been unloaded. The statuesque chestnut colt stood still, yet his long muscles were trembling in his nervousness. Then the crowd moved in, blocking Alec's vision. He heard the high voice of the colt's trainer. "Keep back now! Give him room!"

Alec took the filly away from the fence. It was an ideal time to walk back unmolested to their barn. He and Henry had a lot of routine jobs and unpacking to do this afternoon. "Come on, girl," he said. "We'll see enough of this track all next week."

Alec left without catching another glimpse of Golden Vanity. This was the beginning, *Derby Day minus eight.*

# *Derby Week*

## 17

Shortly after dawn the next morning Alec took the filly for a mild gallop to chase away any travel stiffness left in her legs. They were the first on the track, although the stable area rang to the shouts of grooms, whose work for the day had already begun.

Black Minx galloped easily, seemingly as much at home here as on the training track at home. The Derby racing strip was in excellent condition; there was no jar from the springy cushion as her feet sped over the track. All down the home-stretch and partially around the first turn they passed the great stands, their empty seats looming ever backward. Down the backstretch went the filly and her rider, passing the endless barns, and speeding through air that was thick with wood smoke from the small fires in makeshift stoves and metal drums. As they went around the back turn and passed the stands again, Alec glanced at the presentation stand, where next Saturday's Kentucky Derby winner would go. Here was the Derby winner's circle—the goal of every breeder, trainer, owner, and jockey in the sport!

Henry was still standing at the track gate when they finished. He took the filly's bridle and led her back to their barn. When Alec dismounted, the trainer said, "I'll cool her out. You get your breakfast."

Alec walked through the busy stable area, his jacket collar up and his hands in his pockets, for the spring morning air was brisk. Like the filly, he was beginning to feel a little more at home at Churchill Downs. A good night's sleep on his stable cot had been a help. Henry had slept in the barn too, for they weren't hiring any extra help, and would take care of the filly themselves. This meant that at least one of them must always be near her, for the stakes in the Derby were high.

After Alec had bought a morning newspaper, he went into the stable area's cafeteria. It was crowded but he saw no one he knew—perhaps because he didn't look very hard. After choosing a breakfast of cereal, eggs, and bacon, he carried it on a metal tray to a table.

He read the paper while he ate. There was a large picture of Golden Vanity with his trainer, taken just after their arrival the day before. The colt's trainer was young and smiling. He looked most confident, as if he had great visions of winning not only the Kentucky Derby, but every other important race that year. Yet his statement to the press was modest. "I know Golden Vanity ran a fast race at Keeneland, and we're happy to be here for the Derby." *A little too modest,* Alec thought. *A little too confident.*

He read the rest of the story on Golden Vanity, which

told of his past achievements that made him the red-hot Derby favorite. But there was only one paragraph that really interested Alec. The writer said, "It's been said by many of us that before acclaiming this chestnut colt as one of the finest young three-year-olds of all time, we should wait until another horse is at his head, pushing him through the stretch. Golden Vanity has shown great speed up to a mile and an eighth, and has never given any indication he couldn't go farther. It might well be that there's no horse around that can get up there to look him in the eye and push him in the stretch."

Alec turned to other news of horses and trainers and owners. At no other time of the year would newspapers devote as much space to the racing world as they would between now and the Derby. The horse was king! The eyes of the nation had turned upon Churchill Downs, and readers were eager for stories of the Derby hopefuls.

Wintertime and Lady Lee had arrived late the day before, and their pictures were there, along with those of Eclipse and Silver Jet and stories of their latest works. Alec read them all. Then, turning a page, he saw the headline DERBY SURPRISE COMES EARLY—BLACK MINX.

There was no picture of her, but the columnist wrote:

> The Derby wouldn't be the exciting classic it is if we didn't know that almost anything can happen during the running of the race and if there weren't some *surprise entries* showing up on the grounds the week before. We call them "Cinderella" horses, since most of these colts do not have the back-

ground to make us think of them as serious
Derby contenders, yet they all have great as-
pirations to win the rich classic.

This year's first surprise entry arrived yesterday—a Derby *filly* named Black Minx. Before you stop reading this column at my
mention of a filly and the Derby in the same
sentence, let me hasten to assure you that
this filly rates your attention and consideration. Not because of her past races, since she
ran only once as a two-year-old in Florida
and broke Hialeah's rail and Nino Nella's
collarbone in that outing. (Yes, the same
Nino Nella who's up on the Derby favorite,
Golden Vanity!) Neither does she bear
watching because of her appearance. She's
not exactly small but looks so compared to
the big Derby colts stabled near her. And her
tail is false; she lost her own in a barn accident as a yearling. The one she now wears is
a strange mixture of black and gray, practical
but not beautiful.

However, you can disregard her size and
racing background, and remember the following facts. This filly is a product of Hopeful Farm, home of the Black and Satan. She
is owned and trained by the veteran Henry
Dailey. She is by the Black and out of the
well-bred mare Elf, giving her a pedigree to
match any of the Derby's top candidates. She
is being ridden by the young and skillful
Alec Ramsay, who rode the Black and Satan

in some of their greatest races.

We couldn't get much out of Henry Dailey yesterday on his arrival. He still wasn't certain he'd send his filly to the Derby post. He said, "If she continues to improve this week she'll deserve a chance at the Derby. If she goes, it'll be the first time I've ever tried to win the classic with a maiden."

A lot of *if*'s. But hope springs eternal at this time of year, and it's no different with the horsemen who turn up with Derby surprises. No expert can say that Black Minx, or any other of the lesser lights, "doesn't belong" in the coming classic. Anything can happen in the Kentucky Derby, as has been proven more than once.

Alec left the cafeteria. When he arrived at Barn 10 Henry had finished cooling out the filly and she was back in her stall. Alec handed Henry the morning paper. "You can read this while you eat," he said. "There's a story on the filly."

Henry grunted. Taking the paper, he started down the road.

Alec had a few jobs to do but they were not urgent. His late mornings and afternoons would be spent mostly in waiting and watching. But the days would pass only too fast and before he knew it Henry would be saying, *"You'll go in the Derby with her"* or *"I guess it had better be the Oaks, Alec."* It would be either race . . . the Oaks on Friday or the big one on Saturday. He could only ride her as he was told, and await Henry's decision.

Sunday morning he galloped her again. On Monday, as

they went to the track a little later than usual, Henry said, "Work her a half this morning, Alec. Then gallop out a mile."

This was Derby day minus five, and the number of people standing on the backstretch rail had grown with the increased number of horses appearing on the track. Alec walked the filly through the entrance gate to the track, conscious of the many eyes upon them. He saw that the "dogs" were up, wooden sawhorses placed along the inside of the track to keep the horses away from the rail and to prevent marring the fast cushion that was ready for the afternoon's races.

Henry was still beside them. "Jog her up a way," he said. "Then come back here to me."

Alec stood in his stirrups as he sent the filly into a jog. He kept her near the outside rail. Golden Vanity came down the center of the track, working fast. Nino Nella was "blowing him out," for the chestnut colt was to race the following day in the Derby Trial, the last preparatory race for Saturday's classic.

Before Alec could turn the filly down the track three more Derby colts flashed by, all going at a fast working clip. They were Eclipse, Silver Jet, and Olympus—the last being another surprise Derby entry. Eclipse and Silver Jet were ridden by exercise boys, for their veteran riders—Ted Robinson and Dan Seymour—had not yet arrived at Churchill Downs.

On the way back to Henry, Alec heard the clicking of stopwatches as reporters standing on the rail timed the Derby colts. Alec smiled, for gone was the day when Henry could keep the filly's clocking to himself. Everyone would know what she stepped in the morning's work, and it would be reported in the evening papers along with all other clock-ings of Derby horses. He had almost reached the gate when he saw Wintertime step onto the track. The blood bay colt was reportedly going to run in the next day's Derby Trial, meeting Golden Vanity for the second time; but nothing was official yet, for the Trial entries wouldn't close until that night.

Young Billy Watts sat in the saddle, trying very hard to ignore the attention his mount's presence created. As the trainer adjusted the colt's one-eyed blinker hood, a tall, at-tractive young woman stood beside him.

Alec moved Black Minx more to the center of the track and gave her the bit to play with. A short distance more and they'd be at the half-mile post and off. Henry jerked his head toward the reporters who had left the rail to go to Winter-time. Alec winked back at Henry. Were the reporters more interested in Wintertime or in the good-looking young woman—whom Alec had recognized as the owner of the colt? At any rate there would be few watches, if any, on the black filly. He heard one of the reporters say, "We'd like a story and picture of you, Miss Parshall." Alec gave Black Minx the bit. And just before the filly bolted he heard Win-tertime's owner say, "No, thanks. Only pictures of my colt, please."

Alec sat down to ride, whispering into the filly's ear, "Whoa, girl. Whoa!" His hands worked her mouth, for he could do so easily now without taking the bit from her. As she flew down the remaining part of the backstretch, he kept her in the middle of the track and away from the wooden sawhorses. She swept into the turn, her strides coming faster and longer.

If Alec had had any doubts that the filly was in anything but excellent shape he dismissed them now, for she moved faster than ever before. But he knew, too, that the track was lightning fast, and he must allow for that. As he passed the last furlong pole, he wondered how great her speed would have been if this had not been the last furlong of a half-mile sprint but of a mile-and-a-quarter.

He took the bit away from her just after the finish line, then galloped her for another half-mile. She was worked up but was neither sweating nor breathing hard when he turned her around. On the way back to Henry he caught up with Wintertime, who was getting ready for his work.

Billy Watts turned in the colt's saddle. His bright young eyes left the filly for her rider. "You're Alec Ramsay, aren't you?" he asked.

"Yes." The filly moved restlessly away from Wintertime.

"I've heard a lot about you."

"I've heard plenty about you, too," Alec said.

"You've got a real fine horse there."

"So have you." Alec realized that what he had observed of Wintertime on television was all the more obvious now as he sat beside the colt. Wintertime and the filly were of almost identical size and conformation.

Billy Watts was laughing. "We sound like each other's echo. Well, I got to be goin' or the boss will be on me. So long, Alec."

Henry took the filly's bridle at the barn gate. All eyes were on them and one of the reporters asked, "What'd you clock her, Henry? I guess we missed your filly by a few seconds or more."

Henry shrugged his shoulders. "I hardly ever clock my

horses," he said, nodding to the tall young woman who stood with her trainer near the gate. She smiled and nodded back, and Henry knew she understood that she'd helped him outsmart the clockers for one morning, anyway.

That evening the newspapers announced the names of the horses who would go to the post in the Derby Trial the following afternoon.

## Golden Vanity Goes in
## Mile Derby Trial

The Kentucky Derby favorite, Golden Vanity, meets the highly regarded Wintertime and five other hopefuls in Tuesday's $10,000 Derby Trial, last of the prep races for the "Run for the Roses" on Saturday.

Only Wintertime, second to Golden Vanity in last week's Blue Grass Stakes at Keeneland, is expected to give the chestnut Derby favorite any competition over the mile route. Wintertime's stock rose a bit higher in the Derby picture this morning when he worked a very impressive six furlongs. The five other hopefuls going to the post tomorrow will be running for their Derby lives, as each will have to show enough speed to convince his boss that he's worth the thousand-dollar entry fee for the Kentucky Derby. The five colts "on trial" in the Derby Trial are Olympus, Highboy, Purple Heart, Titan, and My Time.

The popular Derby colts, Eclipse and Silver Jet, are by-passing tomorrow's Trial and an opportunity to meet Golden Vanity before Saturday's classic. However, their trainers agreed to have their colts worked between races in the interest of the afternoon fans who want to see them in action.

When Ray Park, trainer of Golden Vanity, learned of the public works scheduled for Eclipse and Silver Jet, he commented, "I feel that if you're going to work a horse in the afternoon you might better put him in a race and get paid for it." Not too impractical, at that! So tomorrow Golden Vanity stands to pick up another $10,000.

Alec put the newspaper to one side and turned to Henry, who was stretched out on his cot with his eyes shut. "It's getting close," he said.

"Sure is," Henry replied, without opening his eyes. "They tell me the downtown hotels are becoming jammed, and that more people are arriving every day. Some of the guys are griping because the prices of everything have doubled. But what do they expect, with the biggest sports event in America about to take place? They're not being overcharged any more than they'd be any place else with something like this going on. Anyway, folks like to gripe about being overcharged, so they make up stories to take back home. Most of it is just talk, nothing else."

"I wasn't thinking of that side of the Derby," Alec said quietly.

Henry opened his eyes for a moment to look at Alec. "Y'mean tomorrow's Trial? Yeah, it could be interesting. Wintertime was pretty sharp out there this morning."

The room was quiet for several minutes. The filly nickered in the next stall. Alec said, "The Derby Trial is due tomorrow, and the last real works for all of us are soon coming up. It's getting so close I can feel it on my neck."

"Not nervous, are you, Alec?" Henry asked. Then he grinned. "Not an old veteran like you?"

"Sure I am. Why not? *This is the Derby.*"

Henry closed his eyes. "I know it is."

"Have you decided anything yet? Will it be the Derby for her, Henry? Or the Oaks?"

"Give me until Wednesday, Alec."

"Wednesday? Why?"

"I'm going to let you go in a six-furlong race with her that day. Such a short race won't be much of a prep for the Derby but she needs a start to get rid of some of her nervousness." Henry's eyes were still closed. He didn't know Alec was on his feet. "We'll see how she acts, and then we can decide if it will be the Derby or the Oaks for her. We're in no hurry. We've got until Thursday night when the entries close for the Oaks. That's all."

Alec said nothing more, but he stayed on his feet until Henry's deep breathing convinced him his friend was fast asleep. *"That's all,"* Henry had said, as if there wasn't anything more to it.

Alec went out for a long walk.

# *The Derby Trial*

## 18

Tuesday morning was heavily overcast and Alec heard much talk of how a muddy racing strip might affect the results of the Derby Trial. It was well known that Golden Vanity preferred a dry track to a wet one. Continued bad weather would also be a factor in Saturday's Kentucky Derby.

Alec galloped the filly two miles, and none of the other Derby colts did more than that. Most of them would be racing that afternoon, and for Eclipse and Silver Jet there would be the public works. Dan Seymour and Ted Robinson arrived from New York, ready to spend the rest of Derby Week with their mounts. Seymour galloped Silver Jet with the ease and experience of one accustomed to riding many a Derby favorite. He had won three Kentucky Derbies, and on Saturday he would be out for his fourth win in ten years.

Ted Robinson galloped Eclipse with the same quiet air of confidence as Seymour. He, too, had won three Derbies and wanted to make it four on Saturday. But unlike Seymour, who appeared wearing an ancient sweater and breeches which had seen many a morning work, Robinson wore new black breeches, as gleaming as his boots, a white turtleneck sweater and no hat. His heavy black hair was brushed back, as slick and well groomed as the rest of him. He made a lot of money riding horses, and looked it. Seymour made as much money, but didn't look it.

Lady Lee, along with the other fillies who would race in Friday's Kentucky Oaks, worked a fast mile. Alec watched her closely, knowing she'd have the race all to herself if Black Minx didn't go in the Oaks.

"Our filly would give her a real run," he told Henry on the way back to the barn.

"I think we'd beat her," Henry said.

The expected rain didn't fall and by noon there were reports from the track that the bleacher stands already had begun to fill. After lunch Alec returned to their barn to find Henry with a group of old friends who had arrived in Louisville for Derby week. After Alec spoke with them for a while, he went to the filly.

As he groomed her, he told himself that she alone seemed to understand how he felt about the coming Derby. Henry was at home here, as much as he would have been at Hopeful Farm. Henry took it all in stride, becoming, if anything, more likable and more sociable. For Alec it was just the opposite. He wanted to be alone, except for Henry's and the filly's company.

"Good girl," he said. "Good girl." She shook her small head as if she understood his anxiety. He pulled up the blanket a little more around her neck. He fooled with the buckle—loosening the neck strap, and then tightening it again—and all the time she remained still except for an occasional movement of her hoofs in the straw.

He stayed with her a long while, more at ease there than he'd be any other place. He heard the burst of stable activity and he knew what it meant—some of the horses were on their way to the other side of the track, to the paddock, where they'd be saddled for the first race of the afternoon. Later he heard the wafting sound of the bugle calling them to the post. Still later came the sharp roar of the crowd as the horses went off, then the ever-mounting screams until they died off. The winner of the first race had swept beneath the wire!

Alec stayed with Black Minx through still another race and then he heard Henry calling. Going to the stall door, he found the white-haired trainer sitting on a tack trunk, his bowlegs swinging together and then apart. His friends were still with him.

"Will you be here for a while, Alec?" Henry asked. "We want to watch Eclipse and Silver Jet work between the next few races."

"Sure, I'm not going any place."

Henry slid his bulky body off the trunk. "I'll get back in time for you to see the Trial."

"Okay. I'd like to see it."

Alec left the stall to take Henry's seat on the trunk. He watched Henry and his friends go to the next barn to see Silver Jet. The tall gray colt was outside, already bridled and wearing his dark blinker hood. He never wore his hood on the days he was galloped slowly. He had learned that the hood meant business, so now he was moving sideways and on his toes.

Tom Flint stood beside his colt, and Henry spoke to him, introducing his friends. When Silver Jet was saddled Dan Seymour appeared, wearing the same old clothes he had worn during the morning gallop. It made no difference to the veteran jockey that thousands of people would be watching from the stands. Their eyes should be on the colt, not on him.

After Flint boosted the jockey into the saddle, he led the gray colt toward the track. Henry and his friends moved with the rest of the crowd to watch Silver Jet's public work between races.

As Alec watched all this activity, he felt the filly's muzzle against his neck. Her head was pushed far over the stall door and he turned to stroke it. "A lot of people will be naming the Kentucky Derby winner before this day is over," he thought. "They'll see the Big Four in action in one afternoon and will make up their minds about the probable winner of Saturday's race."

He heard the shouts from the crowd and knew Silver Jet had begun his public work. The colt was to go a mile and an eighth in his last long speed trial before the Derby. Would Seymour urge him to top speed? Or would the jockey hold him snug? What would the time be? The track was fast. A few more minutes and he'd know the answers to most of these questions.

The stands were quiet, the people in them just watching now. Alec heard the long beat of Silver Jet's hoofs as he came into the backstretch. The sounds grew ever softer until the beat died away completely, and Alec knew the gray colt was on the far turn. He heard the hoofs again from far across the track as Silver Jet went down the homestretch. There was a tremendous clapping as the work ended. A few minutes later an announcement came over the track's loudspeakers.

"Silver Jet worked the mile and an eighth in one minute forty-nine and two-fifths seconds, and galloped out a mile and a quarter in two minutes and four seconds."

There was another roar from the stands—most of the people knew, as Alec did, that the average Derby winner's time was 2:04! Silver Jet's work had given them a lot to shout about, for he had not gone the last eighth of a mile at top speed. It was obvious that he could do better than 2:04, if he were urged.

Alec saw Henry in the group which followed the gray colt back to the barns, and called to him. "How'd he look?" he asked when his friend reached his side.

"You heard the time, didn't you?"

"Sure," Alec said, "but how did he do it?"

"Easy. Seymour didn't have a strong hold on him most of the way, but he didn't push him, either." Henry jerked his head toward Silver Jet's barn. "Flint just admitted that his colt is in better shape than he was in Florida. This is more than Flint expected and he's beaming like he'd already won the Derby."

Henry stayed with Alec through the running of the next two races, but when Eclipse was taken from the barn for his public work the trainer left again.

Alec watched the saddling activity going on around Eclipse. The brown colt moved uneasily, throwing a hoof at the tightening of his saddle. His white face, raised high above the people near him, was turned toward the track. As Eclipse whistled once, Alec looked up the road, where he saw the blanketed Golden Vanity being led through the gate. The chestnut colt was on his way to the paddock for the Derby Trial.

Alec looked up at the dark sky. He hoped it wouldn't rain before Eclipse had finished his work and Golden Vanity had raced in the Trial. Like everyone else, he wanted to compare the times made by each of the Big Four over the same kind of track.

Ted Robinson appeared at the next barn. Henry was talking to "Red" Dawson, Eclipse's trainer, but he stepped back to let Dawson boost Robinson into the brown colt's saddle. The jockey, like Seymour, was hatless and wearing his morning outfit—the black pants and boots, and the white turtleneck sweater.

Soon they were on their way to the track, and once more Alec had nothing to do but wait.

The roar of the crowd came within a short time. Eclipse had started his work. Seconds later Alec heard the beat of his hoofs as he went around the track. Then came the applause from the stands. Once more there was silence while the announcer said over the loudspeaker, "Eclipse worked a mile and an eighth in one minute and fifty-one seconds, and galloped out the mile and a quarter in two minutes and six seconds."

The applause wasn't as thunderous as it had been for Silver Jet. Alec was certain the white-faced colt had been held under wraps by Robinson. Eclipse was sharp enough to go seconds faster than he had in his public work.

Henry confirmed this upon his return to the barn. "The colt was held back during the whole work. Dawson told Robinson he wanted a two-minute-six mile and a quarter, and the jock gave it to him right on the nose. Robinson has a clock for a head. He's a good boy." Henry pulled Alec off the tack trunk. "You get going now. I've been having all the fun. Give me a good account of the Trial. No, on second thought, never mind. I know what's going to happen, all right."

Alec didn't bother asking questions. He'd heard the call to the post a few minutes before and knew the horses should be at the starting gate. He ran up the road, wondering where he'd be able to get the best view of the Derby Trial.

Nearing the track, he saw hundreds of men from the stable area standing along the rail of the backstretch. There was no place there where he could get near enough to watch the race. He looked around at the barn roofs, already crowded with grooms and boys, and went to the one nearest him. Climbing upon a sawhorse, he reached for the roof. "You got room for one more?" he asked the men sitting on the edge.

Grudgingly they moved over, making room for him, and he pulled himself up. He centered his attention on the backstretch and on the chute which extended beyond the stable area. The mile Trial would start in that chute, giving the horses more than a half-mile of straightaway before they reached the far turn and headed for home. The long-stretch run was ideal for Golden Vanity. With his speed there was no doubt that the colt would take command of the race before rounding the only turn in the mile Derby Trial.

The activity going on behind the starting gate meant that all the horses were not yet in their stalls. Alec couldn't distinguish the horses and riders from where he sat, for he had no binoculars. Although he was at Churchill Downs, actually watching the race, he could not see the start as well as he could have seen it on the television screen at home. He knew Golden Vanity was on the outside post position. But being on the outside was no handicap today, not with the long-stretch run. He knew Wintertime was in number 3 stall, but it looked empty, so the blood bay colt must be one of the horses still behind the gate.

Alec looked across the track. More seats in the gigantic stands were occupied than on any of the previous days, but only the Kentucky Derby would strain the seating capacity of Churchill Downs until it burst and overflowed into the infield. He turned to the still overcast sky. There'd be no rain to hinder Golden Vanity's race now. It was too late. They'd be off any second.

All the colts were in the gate. The doors had closed, and the crowd was silent, waiting for the break. Suddenly the doors were opened!

Alec rose to his feet to get a better view of the start, but the men behind him pulled him down so they could see. He saw Golden Vanity coming on the outside, already a length in front of the field. Nino Nella was urging the colt, leaving no doubt that he wanted to get out in front fast. The jockey's gold-colored silks, as bright and shining as the colt's body, were easy to distinguish in the field. Nella's hands and feet were moving all the time, and as the horses neared Alec the chestnut colt was well over two lengths ahead.

They thundered out of the chute and onto the backstretch of the main track. As they passed, Alec saw Wintertime, on the rail, move out of the pack and go after Golden Vanity. Billy Watts wasn't urging the blood bay colt yet. He sat hugging his mount's neck, his head close to the one-eyed blinker hood that Wintertime wore.

Alec pounded his knee with his clenched fist. He wanted Wintertime to get up there, to catch the flying chestnut leader. But as the horses reached the middle of the backstretch, Golden Vanity continued to pull away from Wintertime and the others.

There was no doubt that the Derby favorite had blazing, blinding speed, for going into the far turn he was four lengths ahead of Wintertime and there was no easing up of his great strides. Like everyone else, Alec remained quiet; he realized that he was watching not a mile race, but an exhibition of extreme speed by Golden Vanity.

In the middle of the turn Billy Watts went for his whip. Wintertime responded to his jockey's urging and for a few seconds it seemed that he narrowed the gap. But going into the homestretch with a quarter of a mile to go, Golden Vanity pulled away again to add another length to his lead. When Wintertime went wide on the turn, Alec knew the Derby Trial was as good as over.

Perhaps Billy Watts knew the chase was futile too, for he put his whip aside and hand-rode Wintertime down the homestretch.

The spectators were almost quiet in their respect for Golden Vanity's great speed as he swept beneath the finish wire, five lengths on top. They watched Nino Nella take up a snug hold on the flying chestnut at the end of the race and go another quarter of a mile. Wintertime also worked the full Derby distance.

A few minutes later the Derby Trial winner came back to a tremendous ovation from the fans. But they ceased applauding Golden Vanity when the announcer said, "Your attention, please. Golden Vanity has broken the track record for a mile."

The crowd roared; then it was quiet again as the announcer went on. "His time for the mile was one minute thirty-five and one-fifth seconds."

More shouts, then everybody was quiet again.

"He went on to a mile and an eighth under a snug hold in one minute forty-nine seconds, and ran out a mile and a quarter in two minutes four seconds!"

Golden Vanity's time for the Derby distance equaled that of Silver Jet's work, *yet the chestnut colt had been held under tight rein from a mile on.* Two minutes four seconds would win most Derbies—but not the one to be raced on Saturday; that much was certain.

Alec got to his feet while the announcer was giving Wintertime's clockings to the stands. The blood bay colt had galloped out his mile and a quarter in 2:05. Alec climbed down from the roof, realizing that like everyone else he had been tremendously impressed by Golden Vanity's blazing speed over the mile route. The chestnut colt had won the Derby Trial without a fight, without any real opposition from Wintertime. It had been that easy. And Nino Nella had been practically standing in his stirrup irons when the colt had gone on to work the full Derby distance.

What was going to happen when Nella really sat down to ride during that last quarter-mile of the Derby? Golden Vanity had just sprinted a full mile in new record time. Could he really carry that kind of speed another quarter of a mile? If so, nothing could catch him. And, if not, what was going to happen? Alec walked back to the barn, knowing that questions such as these never would be answered until the big race.

He was not alone in his thinking. Throughout the country, those who heard of Golden Vanity's brilliant victory were asking themselves the same questions. And in Louis-ville there was little talk of anything else.

That night Henry attended the annual Derby Trainers' party in a downtown hotel. After dinner the horsemen were asked to give the press their forecasts of Saturday's classic. The trainers were cautious in what they said. The Derby was too close for anything but carefully worded statements. Even Golden Vanity's young trainer was afraid to speak up about his colt's chances of winning. He said, "I think it's going to be a wide-open race. We've got high hopes, that's all."

"Red" Dawson, trainer of Eclipse, remarked, "If Golden Vanity and Silver Jet don't go to the post, we might have a chance."

Tom Flint said of Silver Jet's chances, "I can't say we have the Derby winner in our barn, but we might be close."

Don Conover, Wintertime's trainer, said, "We've been running second so long we feel like a June bridesmaid. It's taken the wind out of our sails, but if we can get a second in the Derby we might be satisfied."

There were three other trainers who said they were count-ing on a lot of rain on Saturday, for their only chances lay in a muddy track. And there were still others—those with sur-prise entries and lesser lights—who repeated the comment of one: "My boss has wanted his colors in the Derby since he was knee-high, so we're here and I guess the boss will be getting up his thousand-dollar entry fee on Friday."

Henry, the last trainer to be called upon, gave the briefest and most accurate statement of all. *"We didn't bring a goat to the Derby,"* he said.

# *First Start*

## 19

The following afternoon, Wednesday, Alec rode Black Minx to the post for the first time. There was no doubt that she knew what was happening. In the paddock she had been extremely nervous, and now on the track Alec had all he could do to keep his seat as she swerved from the post parade, side-stepping quickly.

Henry had not been unduly alarmed by her restless antics in the paddock, for he had expected them. His instructions were, "Just stick with her, Alec, and she'll work all this nervousness out in her first start. She should win easy, but I'm not interested in the results as much as I am in just getting a race out of her."

It was the second race of the afternoon. The great stands weren't crowded with people as they'd been the day before for the Derby Trial. Other than Black Minx, no Derby candidates were to be seen in action. She had been made the favorite in this six-furlong race because she was a possible Derby horse and because of her fast morning works.

The post parade ended. Alec turned the filly down the track with the others, going past the stands in a slow canter. The starting gate was across the track at the head of the backstretch. It would be a short race, three-quarters of a mile, nothing more than a good work for a Derby hopeful.

Alec kept the filly on the outside of the track. One of the two red-coated marshals, riding a track pony, kept near them.

"Need any help with her?" the marshal asked.

"She'll be all right," Alec replied.

Black Minx went sideways again, and Alec felt her mouth reaching for the bit. He knew he wouldn't have any trouble giving her the bit today. She'd grab it as soon as he let her. He kept her down to a canter, waiting for the others to get ahead of him before rounding the first turn. It would be best if they were the last to enter the gate. It would mean that much less of a wait for her.

Nine horses were ahead of him, the filly making a field of ten. Henry had chosen this race because of its good-sized field. The Derby would have a field as large or larger. It would be a good test for Black Minx in company with so many. This was a maiden race, restricted to horses who had never won a race.

Alec let the filly go into a gallop but continued standing in his stirrup irons. She drew alongside a dark bay colt. They were approaching the starting gate. The dark bay was from the same stable as Golden Vanity, and Nino Nella was up on him, wearing the bright gold silks he had flourished in the Trial and would wear in the Kentucky Derby.

Nella turned in his saddle, his boyish face as confident, as cocky as if he were riding Golden Vanity rather than a colt who had never won a race. "That filly's crazy," he said, grinning. "She'll spill you one of these days."

"Sure," Alec said. It was the first time Nino Nella had ever talked to him. The young jockey had been too busy with Golden Vanity to give much thought to a filly who had taken him through the rail more than a year ago. At least, Alec had thought so. But it was apparent now that Nella hadn't forgotten Black Minx.

"I wouldn't want any part of her," the jockey said. "You give me room."

Alec pulled down the filly to a jog, and Nella went on ahead. Alec watched the arrogant little jockey ride toward the gate, his stirrups too short, his rear tilted too high. But the kid could ride, Alec admitted, in spite of his bad seat and brazen confidence. And Nella had good reason for thinking so little of Black Minx's ability and intelligence. A broken collarbone and weeks spent in a cast were nothing to be treated lightly.

Alec patted the filly's neck, trying to calm her down. Yet he liked everything he felt. There was an *eagerness* to her action that no morning work had ever produced. Or was it just plain *nervousness,* the mental strain of parading with other horses and going to the post? Eagerness would mean a quick response from her during the race and would restore his confidence in her. If her new action meant nothing more than nervousness, she might go to pieces in the gate, and it would be the end of any Derby hopes.

He took her forward, for all the others were in their gate stalls. She pricked her ears as an assistant starter took her by the bridle. But she moved ahead for him. Alec leaned down to look at the bandages on her forelegs. At Henry's insistence, she was wearing them as a precautionary measure. If she were to go into the Derby on Saturday, nothing must happen to her legs now.

She was in the gate, and the starter's assistants stopped moving about the framework of the stalls. Alec didn't like his post position, number 5. It put him smack in the middle of the field. He hoped Black Minx would break fast, and get out in front during the long run down the backstretch to the far turn. Three-quarters of a mile was nothing more than a sprint. The gate doors closed. He gave her the bit. There was no place for her to go until the wire door in front opened. Her body was trembling. Was it eagerness to be away? Or nervousness? He'd soon know.

Over the track loudspeakers, the announcer told the crowd, "The horses are at the post."

Alec's eyes were straight ahead. He waited and was ready for the break. He knew Nino Nella and the dark bay colt were in the stall to his left. The line of horses and riders were tense, waiting. Then the long line burst at the sound of the bell and the opening of the gate.

Black Minx was late in her break. She bolted from her stall a half-length behind the leaders. The horses inside came out in the shape of a flying wedge with the number 3 horse in the lead. The horses on the outside pushed over and Alec found himself being squeezed in the back of the wedge. The filly was in full flight now and almost on top of the colts running just ahead of her. The horses were jamming against each other.

Alec sought to take hold of the filly and pull her back. But he was too late. He saw Nino Nella's dark bay being bumped hard by another horse. Then the bay stumbled directly in the filly's path! The rest happened so quickly that Alec never remembered its sequence.

He saw the bay colt start to go down and Nella jump from his saddle. He felt the bay's hind feet glance Black Minx's foreleg, upsetting her. She stumbled and he lost his seat, slipping down to one side with no chance of jumping clear. He pushed himself away from her and hit the track hard, his face buried in the dirt. Legs of other horses flew over him. He felt the shock of a hoof grazing the fiber skull helmet he wore beneath his cap, then another hoof struck his shoulder. It was quiet after that except for the roar of a car's motor close by. The track ambulance was coming through the backstretch gate to get him.

He lay still, fully conscious and realizing it was best not to move until they could reach him. The ambulance arrived and its attendants placed him on a stretcher. He saw Nino Nella standing near the door of the ambulance.

"No, I'm all right," Nella was saying. "I jumped clear and landed on my feet. Nothing touched me."

The rear door of the ambulance closed and the white-coated attendant removed Alec's skull cap and black silk blouse. The siren was loud as it left Churchill Downs and sped through the heavy traffic of Louisville. Alec closed his eyes. He felt no pain. Maybe nothing was wrong. What about the filly? Had she gone down too?

It was hours later that he found out about himself and the filly. X-rays had been taken of his head and body. There was no serious injury—no concussion, no fractures—only a shoulder bruise. The doctors had said he could be discharged immediately but that it would be better if he remained in the hospital overnight. Grudgingly, and at Henry's insistence, he had consented.

The filly was all right. She hadn't gone down, hadn't broken a leg as he'd feared. She was in her stall, and except for a small cut found beneath the bandage of her foreleg she was none the worse for her experience. Henry had a competent man staying with her.

From his hospital bed Alec watched Henry clumsily rubbing the skull cap he had worn in the race. There was a dent in its side, where the hoof had glanced off. He wished Henry would put it away.

Henry said, "We can thank this for saving you from a serious injury."

"Let's forget it," Alec said quietly. "The sooner the better." He paused. "How about Nella's dark bay? Did he break anything when he went down?"

"No. He's all right, and so is Nella. You're the only one who ended up in a hospital. Surprising, too, when you think of what a mess it was. We're lucky all around."

"If you hadn't put bandages on the filly's forelegs, we wouldn't have been so lucky," Alec said. "The bay's hoof would have crippled her."

"Yeah, I know."

"Is she putting her weight on the leg?"

"Oh, sure," Henry said. "She'll be perfectly okay tomorrow, and we'll walk her to get any stiffness out."

"That takes care of tomorrow, but what about Friday? Is she going in the Oaks, Henry?"

The trainer shook his head. "No, it'll be the big one, Alec."

The room was quiet for a long while. At last Alec said, "I'd like to get out of here tonight. No sense in my sticking around. They've taken all the pictures they're going to."

"They're thinking about shock, Alec. It wasn't a nice kind of a spill."

Alec grimaced. "I've taken them before. So have a lot of other guys, Nino Nella included."

"He's telling everyone that the filly's a jinx to him."

Alec smiled. "Maybe the jinx will work in the Derby."

"Maybe it will."

"Henry?"

"Yeah?"

"What made you decide it'd be the Derby for her? We didn't do very well out there this afternoon."

"Sure you did," Henry insisted. "Didn't I tell you?"

"Didn't you tell me what? You said she hurdled the bay colt when he went down and didn't hurt herself, but that's all."

Henry tapped the sides of his chair with his boots, and for a second it was the only sound in the small room. Then he said, "She not only hurdled him, but went on to finish 'way in front of the winner of the race."

Alec chewed his lower lip. Then he asked, "You mean she raced all by herself, that she didn't quit?"

Henry nodded. "'Course she was running away again, knowing she'd gotten rid of you. But as you say, she didn't quit like she could have done. That's good enough for me." He got to his feet, his steel gray eyes brighter, and moved toward the door. "The track marshals had an awful time catching her. She led them a merry chase around the track, goin' up and down the stretches, always slipping around them, before they finally caught up with her. She must have gone a couple of miles all told. She's got the stamina and the speed. She sure deserves a chance at the Derby."

Henry stopped at the door. "At the time I wasn't much interested in what she was doin'. You and the ambulance had pulled off the track and I could only think about you until I got here and found everything all right. Now it's different. I can think about her now."

"Sure," Alec said. "You've got a Derby horse."

"And a Derby rider. You get some sleep, Alec. It's the first good bed you've had in a week."

Alec smiled. "Well, when you put it that way . . ."

" 'Night, Alec."

"See you in the morning, Henry."

When the door was closed, Alec's face sobered. To himself he said, "Tomorrow, Friday, then *Saturday*." He closed his eyes and tried not to hear the lurching of a horse's body above his head, the dull, sickening thud of an aluminum-shod hoof. He had only two days to forget. He opened his eyes to see the dented skull cap, still on the chair where Henry had left it. He looked at it a long while, knowing that it was far better to accept it than to turn away and forever fear it.

*Derby Day minus two.*

# Derby Day

## 20

When Alec reached the track early Thursday morning, most of the Derby colts had finished their gallops. He found Henry in Napoleon's stall, cleaning it and muttering to himself while he worked. Alec knew the reason for Henry's grumbling, for the morning paper, lying on the tack trunk, was opened to a page on which there was a picture showing Black Minx being chased by the two track marshals. The caption over the picture read, HENRY'S GOAT.

Alec had read the story in the taxi on the way to the track. The writer had made good use of Henry's comment at the Trainers' Dinner on Tuesday night. He claimed Henry might have brought a goat to the Derby at that, since *"Black Minx displayed the agility of a goat in her first start yesterday by hurdling one fallen horse and evading the track marshals for all of ten minutes before she tired and they were able to corner her."*

Henry left Napoleon when he saw Alec, and after a few

minutes together they went toward the filly's stall. "I think I'll ride Napoleon out with you when you go to the Derby post," Henry said. "It might make things a little easier for her if she's got the old boy for company." He didn't explain if "old boy" meant Napoleon or himself, and Alec didn't ask.

Alec glanced at the filly's right foreleg when they entered her stall. There seemed to be nothing wrong except for a slight scratch above the fetlock.

Henry said, "She's a little stiff. I was waiting for you to walk it out of her."

Black Minx pushed her head onto Alec's chest and he smoothed out her forelock until it hung between her large eyes. Sure she'd be stiff. His shoulder was a little stiff, too. They were lucky there wasn't anything more serious the matter with them.

Henry glanced outdoors. It was a gray morning, with a soft drizzling rain. "If this weather keeps up it'll make the 'mudders' happy. They'll go in the Derby if it's a heavy track."

"Did Golden Vanity gallop this morning?" Alec wanted to know.

"Sure. He'll go on a muddy track but nobody in his stable will like it."

"It's only Thursday. We have two days for the rain to stop."

"Yep, but it could get worse."

"She wouldn't like a muddy track either," Alec said of the filly.

"No, but she'd go," Henry returned. He left the stall to get Black Minx's bridle and saddle, for the drizzle had suddenly ceased and it was a good time to get her out.

Alec removed her blanket. "We sure made a great beginning yesterday," he told her softly. "But anyway, you got your picture in the papers. You did that, all right."

They had the track pretty much to themselves in their two-mile walk and jog that morning. Alec felt better for the exercise and he figured the filly felt the same. He rubbed her down well and spent the rest of the day with Henry. Like everyone else now, they were just waiting for Saturday.

To the joy of some stables and the disappointment of others, Friday turned out to be clear with the promise of a hot, dry day. Before the sun came up Alec had Black Minx on the track with all the other Derby horses, most of whom were blown out in their last fast breezes before racing in the classic. But Henry had Alec keep the filly to a slow gallop.

The backstretch rail and stable area were crowded with early risers who had come to watch. But the men who trained, owned, and rode the Derby horses paid little attention to anything but their charges. For months, and for a few of them years, they had pointed their colts for the classic to be raced the afternoon of the following day. They watched their Derby hopefuls with level, steely gazes, knowing that within a few hours they must decide whether or not they should pay the thousand dollars necessary to start in the Derby. They talked little, smiled little. The reporters were told brusquely to write their own stories. The horsemen would have nothing further to say until five o'clock the next afternoon, at the finish of the Derby.

As Alec rode Black Minx back to the barn, with Henry at her head, some of the reporters made reference to "Henry's

Goat" in an attempt to get the trainer to make a comment. Henry said nothing.

All the rest of the morning and during the afternoon, photographers were everywhere about the stable area, taking their last-minute pictures for the next day's papers. During all this activity Henry and Alec stayed close to Black Minx, never leaving her for a moment, not even to go to the track during the afternoon to watch the running of the Kentucky Oaks. But they heard the announcement of the results over the loudspeakers. Lady Lee had won easily in new record time for the filly classic. Wet and shining in all her newly won glory, she came back to the stable area surrounded by her admirers and the press.

Henry said, "She sure deserved to win. A fine filly, just as game as they come. She'd make a wonderful broodmare for the farm, if we could ever get hold of her."

Alec caught a glimpse of Lady Lee's small and dapper owner, who was trying to keep the crowd back from his filly. "I don't think we could buy her," he said.

Later in the day Henry left for the Secretary's office to enter Black Minx in the Kentucky Derby. And that evening the papers carried the names of the horses in the Derby field and their post positions. The list was sent to the nation over the wire services and radio.

## KENTUCKY DERBY FIELD

Here is the field for tomorrow's $100,000 added Kentucky Derby, showing post positions, owners, trainers and jockeys. Gross value if 10 start is $116,500. All weights 126 pounds except for lone filly, Black Minx, allowed 5 pounds, carrying 121.

| Post Position | Horse | Owner | Trainer | Jockey |
|---|---|---|---|---|
| 1 | Olympus | Circle Ranch | A. Moore | F. Smith |
| 2 | Eclipse | Brookside Stable | R. Dawson | T. Robinson |
| 3 | Rampart | James Hine | S. Potter | J. Stokes |
| 4 | Silver Jet | Thomas Flint | T. Flint | D. Seymour |
| 5 | *Black Minx | Henry Dailey | H. Dailey | A. Ramsay |
| 6 | Golden Vanity | Lionel Graham | H. Park | N. Nella |
| 7 | Break-up | Queen Ranch | T. Gregory | M. Jones |
| 8 | Lone Hope | Powder Mill Stable | D. Hunt | J. Cornwell |
| 9 | Wintertime | Jean Parshall | D. Conover | W. Watts |
| 10 | My Time *filly | Mona Stable | J. Grim | L. Henney |

Alec went over the list with Henry. They knew that Olympus, Rampart, and Lone Hope, like Black Minx, were the untried and lightly regarded surprise entries who would definitely go to the Derby post with the Big Four, making eight starters certain. Break-up and My Time were "mudders" and most likely would go only if it rained and the track was heavy.

Alec finally left the stall to walk about the stable area. The exercise didn't help very much to relieve his nervousness. They had a fair post position, he told himself, away from the rail yet not too far outside. He caught himself thinking that number 5 had been their post position in Wednesday's ill-fated race. He dismissed it from his mind, not wanting to remember it.

Returning to the barn, he went to Black Minx. He stayed with her for a while and then left, afraid that his Derby-eve jitters might only be communicated to her and make things worse. He returned to Henry to find his friend already stretched out on his cot, his eyes closed. Alec envied his friend's ability to lie still, perhaps even to sleep.

He picked up the newspaper again. There was little space that wasn't devoted to the Kentucky Derby. He read, knowing he might as well accept the fact that *the day* was about here, that it did no good to try to escape it, that it might help more if he jammed his head full of Derby news until he was numb from it all. He might be able to sleep then.

He read everything. He learned that the majority of turf writers rated Golden Vanity as "the horse to beat if the track is fast for the Derby." Nevertheless, the readers were advised to watch what might happen "if Silver Jet gets near enough to Golden Vanity in the stretch run to look him in the eye."

The race prophets were being cagey with their forecasts, and their stories and comments were crammed with *if*'s and *but*'s. Readers were also asked to remember that Eclipse was sharper than he had ever been.

As one writer said, "We must disregard his loss to Silver Jet in the Wood Memorial, when he was plagued with bad racing luck. If he hadn't been bumped going into the far turn, the results of that race might have been different. Wintertime should be kept in mind as well, for he is stronger than his small size indicates. Also, he's a stretch runner as proven in his losing races to Eclipse in Experimental Number Two and to Golden Vanity in the Blue Grass Stakes, and again in last Tuesday's Derby Trial. He was holding his own coming down the stretch in every race, and there's no telling what might happen in that last long furlong of the Derby."

Nor did the experts ignore the possibility of a victory by one of the lesser lights. Olympus, Rampart, and Lone Hope had shown some remarkable morning works, and "they're unraced and untried, but anything can happen in the Derby."

*Anything can happen in the Derby.* Alec smiled. How often

had he heard it and read it this week. It provided an easy "out" for the turf writers, trainers, owners, and jockeys alike.

Black Minx was worthy of attention too, the sportswriters acknowledged. "A dangerous combination at any racetrack at any time are Hopeful Farm's trainer, Henry Dailey, and the farm's rider, Alec Ramsay. Although their filly, Black Minx, is not being given much consideration in some quarters, she bears watching. After all, a filly did win *one* Derby!"

Tiring of the prophesies, which were nothing more than carefully worded comments to cover almost any kind of a result in the big race, Alec turned to news of activities going on downtown.

All hotels were full, and now people were overflowing into towns within a radius of one hundred miles of Louisville. It was estimated that more people would be at Churchill Downs the next day than ever before. One Derby visitor had taken over a large highway motel for himself and his sixty guests. Special trains sided in the Louisville stations made up what was being referred to as "Railroad Town." Thousands were making their homes in the trains while awaiting the Derby. One special train was from Texas, and its occupants were feasting on six hundred Texas steaks they had brought with them.

Alec continued reading for a long time, finding these stories more relaxing. It was almost midnight when his eyes became heavy and he decided that he could now sleep. He turned off the light, but it was another hour before he actually slept.

It was no better the next morning, and in many ways much worse. He galloped the filly but it didn't help. Even though the sun was not yet up, the gates to Churchill

Downs were open and the bleacher stands on the turns were already packed with people who had stood outside the main entrance all night long. Within a few hours the track's infield would be a great mass of people as well. Only the towering grandstand and clubhouse would be empty until race time, for all seats there were reserved.

The Derby horses finished their gallops and returned to the barns. The stable area lacked the noise of other mornings, the good-natured calls, the whistling, even the humming of the grooms to their charges. The barns were closed to people not directly concerned with the Derby horses. *No visitors today. No hay today. We go to the post at 4:30.*

The sun came up. The sky was cloudless. It promised to be a hot afternoon, with the track fast. The day would be too bad for the "mudders," but good for the others.

Henry wasn't calm any more. All morning long he "stall-walked" up and down the dirt runway before the barn. And other trainers in other barns did the same. Repeatedly Alec went from Henry to the filly, and then back to walk with Henry again. There was nothing to do but wait as he had done all week long. Yet today there would be an end to the waiting.

Noon came. The early races had already begun. The noise from the stands was increasing with each hour. More and more people were arriving. By four-thirty there wouldn't be room to move, to breathe, except for a mile and a quarter of lonely track.

Henry didn't want to eat, so Alec went to the cafeteria alone, but he scarcely touched his food. On the way back to the barn, he passed Billy Watts and nodded. Wintertime's jockey didn't seem to see him, and Alec wondered if his own face looked as white and as grim as Billy Watts's.

He heard the band playing across the track, but never looked in that direction. He would see the track soon enough. Instead, he looked up at the sky, to watch the many planes flying back and forth. Some were pulling long advertising trailers behind them; others were waiting as he was for the classic to begin.

He passed the barns of Silver Jet, Eclipse, Golden Vanity, and Wintertime, and wondered why the colts alone appeared calm and undisturbed. But soon they would know too; they'd know on their way to the paddock.

In their own barn, Henry had his jacket off, and his shirt clung to his body with sweat. He spoke only to tell Alec to stretch out on the cot and relax. For a while Alec tried it; then he got up and went to the filly for some comfort. But he didn't stay very long with her, for she was calm and he decided that he did her no good.

An hour before post time Alec said, "I'd better get going now." He hardly recognized his own voice. He knew he must go to the jockey house to dress and weigh out for the race.

It had come. It was the beginning of the end of all the waiting.

Henry said, "Yes, I guess it's time."

"Have you got someone to take Napoleon across when you bring the filly?"

Henry nodded.

Alec let his hand trail off Black Minx's muzzle. "I'll see you in the paddock, then."

"In the paddock," Henry repeated.

Alec saw nothing, heard nothing, as he walked toward the

track entrance. He was alone. He'd cross the track, the infield, and then go through the underpass to come up near the paddock and jockey quarters in back of the grandstand. The policemen let him through the gate, and he hurried across the track, seeing only the ambulance that was parked at the gate, the one thing he hadn't wanted to see. To forget it he looked beyond to the moving mass of humanity in the infield and stands. Then he lowered his eyes again and kept walking. Soon he and the filly would be on the track. Soon the waiting would be over.

# *The Kentucky Derby*

## 21

Thirty minutes before post time Alec stepped from the official scales and started for the paddock. He stopped on the balcony of the jockey quarters and looked below at the multitude of faces behind the grandstand and clubhouse. All who could get close enough were jammed against the open shed that housed the paddock. The colts and *his filly* were in their paddock stalls, waiting for the call to the post.

Alec carried Black Minx's saddle. It had gone on the scales with him, making up the 121 pounds she'd be carrying on her back as against 126 pounds for the colts. A filly was permitted to carry five pounds less than the colts. Even that wouldn't help her much. Fillies couldn't race a mile and a quarter against colts in the spring of their third year. Fillies didn't win the Derby . . . *only one had won it.*

He started down the stairs in all-black silks and highly polished black boots that shone in the sun's rays. The only thing white on him was the number 5 high on his right shoulder. Other riders moved along near him, but he paid them no attention. Nothing mattered now but the black filly.

Protected from the surging crowd by a high wire-mesh fence, Alec walked with the others through the paddock. In the center of the rectangular building, there were two rows of stalls, built back to back. It was quiet here compared to the world just on the other side of the fence.

Alec passed Olympus, Eclipse, Rampart, and Silver Jet without looking at them. He touched old Napoleon's nose as he circled him and went to the filly in her paddock stall.

Henry took the light saddle from him without a word, and gently put it on top of the saddle cloth that also carried the number 5. As he tightened it, Black Minx moved uneasily beneath the binding girth strap.

Alec glanced quickly about the covered shed. Only the mud horse My Time had been scratched from the race. Break-up, another "mudder," would go in spite of the fast track, making a field of nine.

The television cameras were on a platform at one end of the paddock, and even now were carrying the Kentucky Derby preliminaries to a waiting nation. Alec knew that his mother and father would be watching and waiting for a glimpse of him on the screen. He turned back to the filly. She was beginning to act up a little. Her calmness was gone. She *knew* now, as they did.

Henry stood quietly beside the filly, stroking her, talking to her. But never did he say a word to Alec. His instructions, if any, would come later on the way to the post.

A bell sounded, and the paddock judge called, "Riders up!"

It had come. It was here. Alec moved to the side of the filly. He raised his knee to Henry's cupped hand. Henry tried to grin at him, failed completely, and nodded instead.

As Alec sat in the saddle, his head began to reel. He leaned forward, bringing the blood to his head. He shook it, and heard Henry ask anxiously, "You all right, Alec?"

"Derby jitters," he replied, sitting back in his saddle. "It'll go away now, I think. When we move, it'll go away."

Henry's face was white. "I know," he said. "I didn't eat anything." As if that explained it all.

The colts were beginning to move about the paddock. Number 1, Olympus . . . number 2, Eclipse . . . number 3, Rampart. Silver Jet was taken from the adjacent stall, wearing number 4. Then it was the filly's turn.

Henry mounted Napoleon and led Black Minx out of the stall. Slowly they followed Silver Jet. Behind them came Golden Vanity, Break-up, Lone Hope and, last in the paddock parade, Wintertime, number 9.

The huge crowd pressed closer to the fence, shouting nothings and calling to the jockeys. Alec straightened in his saddle, moving his shoulders to relieve his tension. But his stomach and head were all right. The waiting had ended.

It was the filly who was upset now. She pushed hard against Napoleon in her excitement. The old gray plodded along, his big body rebuffing her jolts, never giving an inch. But Black Minx was no more restless than the colts. All had their stable ponies and trainers beside them. No owner was taking a chance of anything happening to his Derby horse between the paddock and the post.

"*There's Golden Vanity!*" someone shouted outside the confines of the paddock fence. "*Number six.*" He began singing "California Here I Come," and for the chorus was joined by hundreds of other voices.

*"Here we go, Silver Jet! Ride him, Seymour! Bring that gray ghost home!"*

*"Oh, you Eclipse you!"* a girl cried. *"Oh, you Robinson!"*

*"Today's the day, Wintertime!"*

*"Ram home, Rampart!"*

*"There's Henry's goat! Hey, Alec! Move that billy-goat today!"*

*"Filly-goat, you mean!"*

*"Break it up, Break-up!"*

*"You're my Lone Hope!"*

On and on the calls came as the horses circled the paddock shed; the noise ended only when the bugle sounded the call to the post. Most of those in the crowd moved at once, surging beneath the stands to the track, where they would witness the great race.

Alec pulled down his cap more securely about the protective fiber liner beneath it. This was an instinctive movement. He was not thinking of Wednesday's accident. All he was conscious of now was the filly. All that mattered was the race ahead of them. His face was still grim, but a new and comforting calmness flowed through his body. It had come just as it always came when the waiting was over.

They left the covered paddock to walk for a moment in the sun. They went down a fenced runway toward the tunnel which would take them beneath the great stands and to the track. People pressed close to the runway fence, still shouting. But Alec no longer heard them. His eyes remained straight ahead, blinking a little in the bright sunlight. Before they entered the tunnel his gaze swept to the names of previous Kentucky Derby winners lettered along the back of the great stands above.

Henry led the filly into the darkness of the underpass. Just beyond, the sun shone on the track. Eight colts and a filly were going out there. Whose name would be added to that long list? Alec wondered. Which horse would meet the supreme test to come and emerge a champion in this year's Kentucky Derby?

They were coming out of the tunnel now. Olympus, number 1, stepped onto a track turned by the bright sun into the color of flowing gold. And with his strides the band directly across from them began playing "My Old Kentucky Home."

More than a hundred thousand spectators were on their feet yet strangely silent while the strains of the song wafted lingeringly through the still air. The melody was played as the horses filed onto the track, their bodies sleek and beautiful, their riders colorful in bright silks. The crowds in the great stands and centerfield remained quiet, watching the horses, listening to the old and beloved tune.

Alec understood the silence. He felt the music move into his heart, felt it stiffen his spine and prickle the back of his neck. How long ago had he first heard it? In school certainly. Maybe before that from his mother. It was joy. It was sorrow. It was the story of the old South. Long ago he had accepted it as these. Yet even as a child he had thought of barns and foals, of Kentucky and bluegrass and horses. It meant the Derby too. He knew there were tears in his eyes but he didn't care. It was nothing to be ashamed of.

The melody ended and the multitude came to life. The horses turned to the right, to file down the track before a thunderous acclamation. They passed the winner's circle, going beyond and passing the finish line of the Derby. They went as far as the first turn, and then came back up the stretch again—that long, hard boulevard over which they would speed twice before the race ended.

The starting gate was far up the track at the head of the homestretch. They went toward it, still in file, still parading before the stands. Olympus walked directly behind the red-coated, black-capped marshal in the lead.

Eclipse was next, walking quietly and staying close to his stable pony. Ted Robinson was having no trouble with the burly colt. The jockey's maroon-and-white silk-clad body hardly moved in the saddle.

Rampart was quiet too, but Silver Jet was prancing and his black-hooded head was stretched out, demanding more rein from Dan Seymour. In his red-and-black silks the jockey stood in his stirrups and kept a tight rein on his gray mount.

Black Minx tried to get away from Henry and stepped out of line, but Henry moved Napoleon still closer to keep her under control.

Behind them Golden Vanity reared, almost unseating Nino Nella. The crowd shrieked. His trainer got him down and back in line. The Derby favorite walked quickly, his great body impressive and startling in its beauty, and already shining with sweat.

The others in the field—Break-up, Lone Hope, and the red-hooded Wintertime—stayed in line. Except for constant prancing and pushing against their lead ponies, they made no fuss.

The parade ended in the middle of the stretch, and the horses were allowed to step out of line. Some went off in a canter, and others in a trot, but all headed toward the starting gate at the head of the stretch.

Henry kept the filly close to him and, without turning to Alec, gave his instructions. "Keep her back, not too far, if you can help it. If she gets a clear path in front she'll run herself out. I don't think you'll have trouble keeping her back. Golden Vanity is sure to be out front, and maybe Silver Jet with him. The pace will be fast, too fast, I think. So if you can stay behind some other colts do it until the mile post anyway, then get her clear and let her go. She should be able to go the last quarter. The race will be decided there, particularly the last furlong. Watch Eclipse. He's made to go the full distance."

Alec said, "I understand. You want me to keep her back in the field and not worry about the pace up front until the mile post. Is that it?"

Henry nodded. The starting gate was just ahead. He'd be leaving the track soon and turning the filly over to the starter's ground crew.

Alec said, "Golden Vanity might run so far out in front none of us will be able to catch him."

Henry turned in his saddle for the first time to meet Alec's gaze. "If he can hold the rest of you off in that last quarter he'll deserve to win. A horse is game to come from behind but it requires greater gameness, greater courage for a horse to race in front and still repel the challenges he'll surely get in this stretch run. If Golden Vanity can do it, he'll be a champion and a worthy one. That's all, Alec. Here's good luck to both of you." They were in back of the gate. Henry tried to grin but raised his hand instead. He let go of the filly and rode away with the others.

Over the loudspeakers came the announcement, "Ladies and gentlemen, the horses have reached the starting gate."

*We're alone now. Just you and me, girl. Just the two of us.*

He took her halfway around the back turn, farther from

the gate than any of the other colts. *They'll wait for us. It'll mean less time to spend inside.* But finally he turned her back. She whinnied and struck out a foreleg either in play or eagerness, and he thought of the Black at home. She'd never pulled that trick before while in stride. A little of *him* coming out in her.

He kept the bit from her, but her mouth was always reaching for it. He heard the roar of planes flying overhead but never looked at the sky. But above her tossing head he saw the tiers on the roof of the great stands; they were crowded with cameras, even now focused on the horses as they entered the gate.

Wintertime and Lone Hope were still outside their stalls, along with the filly. The rest were inside the gate and waiting. There was a handler for each horse still outside, and one man called, "Hurry up that filly, Ramsay."

The starter, standing on his platform just ahead and to the left of the gate, said, "Don't have him rush her, Milton. No hurry. We've got time. Bring her up slowly, Ramsay. And Watts, you ride Wintertime up slowly too." The starter was making an attempt to be indifferent to the importance of this race. But his sagging grim face betrayed the softness of his voice and his patient instructions. He knew there could be no slips in this start.

The filly's handler took her by the bridle. He looked up at Alec and said, "Shucks, what's the Derby but another hoss race." His face was just as white as the starter's.

She went into her stall without making any fuss. Alec was surprised, even disappointed, that she'd walked so readily inside. He hadn't counted on it. They'd have to spend a few minutes now waiting for Wintertime and Lone Hope to come into the gate. The door behind was shut and the stall quarters were close. The handlers were moving about the framework of the gate, helping riders to keep control of their flighty mounts.

"Nino Nella," the starter called from his platform. "Keep your colt's head up. Help him, Kelley." Golden Vanity was twisting in his stall.

Alec stroked the filly's neck. "Easy, girl. Easy now," he kept repeating.

The television cameras, ready to pick up the start of the classic, were just ahead and off the track. The center field was black with people, like the stands to the right. Only the long stretch was clear, a yellow empty road soon to be filled.

Wintertime and Lone Hope were still outside the gate. Were they having trouble? Or were their riders intentionally making the others wait, hoping nervous gate antics would tire them out?

Alec continued stroking the filly. She was good. She was quiet. It would be all over in a matter of minutes once they left the gate. Two minutes and very few seconds. More than a hundred thousand people had gathered to watch a race that would end in those flashing minutes. Some had been here all week, waiting for it, and still others had waited all year.

But it was no different for the horses. Nine of more than a hundred early Derby nominations had made the post, and now they, too, were waiting.

Wintertime had entered his stall, but Lone Hope was giving his handler trouble and remained outside the gate.

The line to Alec's left was quiet. Olympus was on the rail. He was a light bay, unraced and untried. His jockey was a grim-faced veteran of twelve Derbies who had never had a winner. Maybe this one would be it!

The burly Eclipse was next. He had been one of the top two-year-olds. And this year, at three, he had already won the Experimental Number Two, and had come in second to Silver Jet in the Wood Memorial. Ted Robinson was up, and trying for his fourth Derby win. Young in age, old in experience, he was as nervous now as the rest of them.

Rampart, like Olympus, was untried. But his jockey was another veteran.

Silver Jet, waiting in the stall on the filly's left, had been the champion two-year-old. This year he had won the Flamingo and the Wood Memorial. His rider was Dan Seymour, old in age, old in experience. But the Derby wasn't just another race for him either. One had only to look at him to know.

Golden Vanity was on the filly's right. The Derby favorite, twisting and restless in his stall, seemed anxious to be turned loose. Nino Nella was up and white of face. He looked scared and frightened, no longer cocky.

Break-up, too, had been untried in fast company but he had a competent rider in the saddle.

Lone Hope finally entered the next stall, still fighting his handler and jockey. Another surprise entry; another of the lesser lights!

In the outside stall stood Wintertime, third in Experimental Number One, third in Number Two, second in the Blue Grass Stakes to Golden Vanity, second again to Golden Vanity in the Derby Trial. Billy Watts, in the saddle, was young and frightened.

*Boys became men riding a Derby, or they remained forever boys.*

Alec got ready to go. He let the filly have the bit. The

door had closed behind Lone Hope. There was a deathly silence, except for the voice of the announcer, who said needlessly, "The horses are at the post."

Everyone waited for the break, not wanting to miss a thing that happened during the next two minutes.

The starter was watching Lone Hope, waiting for the colt to settle down now that he was in the gate. He reared and came down to stand still. The starter said, "I'll wait a moment. Let him settle down now." But Alec recognized the ring in his voice. Even as he slapped the filly's neck the bell rang and the doors flew open, freeing the Derby horses.

THEY'RE OFF!

Black Minx jumped first out of the gate along with Silver Jet. But in her eagerness or excitement at being free she broke from Alec's guiding hands and swerved toward Silver Jet. She straightened as her left shoulder hit his right shoulder and bounced off. Startled, she pulled up stride, still lunging in toward him. His heaving flanks struck her on the chest.

Alec felt her take the impact, flinching but never losing her balance. He pulled her away from the gray colt. She steadied, her strides coming smoothly once more. He had her clear of interference now and sat down to ride, moving the reins easily against the corners of her mouth and whispering, "Whoa, girl. Whoa!"

Only Silver Jet was ahead. No other inside horse had broken as fast as the filly. Even Golden Vanity was behind.

His filly had narrowly escaped a fall, but now she was free and full of run! He kept her directly behind Silver Jet, remembering Henry's instructions and hoping that a few other horses would come up to them and go past. He had wanted to get her out near the front at the break. But third or fourth position would be best until the end of a mile.

They were only a few strides from the gate. The first run down the long stretch was just beginning. The stands were a tumultuous roar but Alec heard nothing but the beating hoofs, the straining bodies, all around him.

Golden Vanity was surging up on their right, his great body stretched out, and Nino Nella rocking fast in his saddle. In a burst of blinding speed he passed, catching up to the gray colt ahead.

Alec saw Dan Seymour use his whip once, urging Silver Jet to greater speed and accepting Golden Vanity's early challenge for the lead. The filly picked up her stride too, and Alec's teeth tore his lips. He didn't want her to become involved in the duel of speed that had already begun directly ahead of them. This was only the first quarter-mile of a long race. He regretted getting her out of the gate so fast. Even more, he regretted his inability to hold her back, to rate her and save something for the grueling, punishing end of the race.

She was stretched out in head and legs, and he could do nothing to slow her down except to whisper his *whoa*'s less often, to move the reins less frantically against her mouth. She didn't gain an inch on the flying leaders, but neither did they draw away from her. They passed the finish line for the first time. The crowd's voices shattered the heavens, for the great duel between Golden Vanity and Silver Jet had begun with still a mile to go.

The call came over the loudspeakers, "At the quarter, Silver Jet on top by a nose. Golden Vanity, second. Black Minx, third. Lone Hope, fourth. Eclipse, fifth. Rampart, sixth. Wintertime, seventh. Break-up, eighth, and Olympus, ninth."

Alec heard part of the call, but no other colt could be seen to his left or right. He sent Black Minx closer to the rail, saving ground. He knew she was going all out much too fast, too early. He knew it wasn't the race Henry had planned for them. And he *didn't know* the filly's left foreleg was open and bleeding from a blow by Silver Jet's right hind hoof at the break. If he had known, he would have taken the bit from her, and the Derby would have ended there for them.

They swept into the first turn two lengths behind the leaders, the filly still holding ground despite the furious pace being set for her. Behind, Alec heard the pounding hoofs of the field. A head neared the filly's flanks going into the turn, a red-hooded head, and Alec knew Wintertime was there. The blood bay colt must have come up fast at the end of the stretch run, for he had been seventh.

The filly's strides were made for the turns. She pulled up on the leaders, and Wintertime's head fell back. A length in front of her, Golden Vanity passed Silver Jet, taking the lead from him. But Seymour used his whip once more and the gray colt drew even again with the chestnut favorite.

Alec saw Nella glance in surprise at finding Seymour beside him again. They were entering the backstretch and the sprinting duel was still in progress. Apparently Seymour had instructions to keep Silver Jet with Golden Vanity, to outsprint him, to break him down if he could.

The noise from center field, from the backstretch rail, from the packed roofs of the barns, became a bedlam. Silver Jet was staying with Golden Vanity. Head and head, eye and eye. Here was the duel for which all had hoped but never expected to see!

Alec pressed his head close against the filly's straining neck. He hardly touched the reins or called to her any longer. The terrific pace was suicide for all three of them—the chestnut, the gray, and his filly! No horse could endure a mile and a quarter at such speed. Horses before them had made a sprint of the Derby, but never such a fast and blinding sprint as this! Soon they'd crack beneath the strain and go to pieces. The Derby would be won by some colt now running behind them!

They had gone a half-mile. The call came from the loudspeakers, but Alec couldn't catch the position of the colts in back. It made no difference. He heard Golden Vanity's time called. It was forty-six and one-fifth seconds, *the fastest half-mile in Derby history*! He was more certain than ever that the race was over for all three of the leaders.

In the middle of the backstretch, another colt came up alongside. Alec saw Eclipse's white face at the filly's flanks. He wanted the burly colt to come up closer, to pass, to move in front, and perhaps slow down; he wanted him to keep the filly behind him and compel her to save something for the long race still to be run. But Ted Robinson on Eclipse made no bid to take his colt past. He stayed behind the filly and just outside, content to wait for the homestretch.

Three lengths ahead, the bitter duel between Golden Vanity and Silver Jet was going on. Seymour had his gray colt close to the rail and was now a long neck in front of the chestnut. But just before going into the last turn, Nella made another move. Golden Vanity responded with a tremendous burst of speed. He moved ahead of Silver Jet, flying into the turn on top with the shrill screams of thousands of voices to urge him on.

Silver Jet fell back before this fresh and heartbreaking on-slaught of supreme speed. As the roar of the crowd filled Alec's ears, he felt his filly respond to the terrible challenge ahead. She pounded into the far turn, every muscle straining, and Alec could do nothing to hold her down. Eclipse fell back, Robinson content to wait still longer before making his move.

By the middle of the turn, Black Minx was close to Silver Jet's heaving flanks. Two lengths ahead of them ran the chestnut colt. Golden Vanity was nearing the pole at the head of the homestretch, the end of a mile; he still had a quarter-mile to go down that long, long stretch to the finish line.

Alec kept the filly behind Silver Jet, never giving her a chance to get clear of him. Seymour was hand-riding now. The duel with the chestnut had been lost. The jockey was saving what was left in his gray mount, hoping it was enough to carry him down the stretch, hoping that Golden Vanity couldn't maintain his speed for another quarter of a mile. Alec stayed there, trying to save his mount too.

The pounding of hoofs behind them came ever closer and more thunderous as they swept off the turn and entered the stretch run. Here before them was the actual "Run for the Roses"! Here the colts would struggle down the last quar-ter-mile of the longest run in their young lives! Here was the final testing ground, a great classic to be won or lost!

Suddenly the pack from behind was upon them. Surging heads and bodies stretched far across the track, but still a stride behind. There was a flash of multicolored silks, of flashing whips and spurs. The very ground rocked with the beat of hoofs and the stomping of thousands upon thousands of human feet. The air was filled with the screams of the multitude, deadening the shrill cries of the jockeys.

Seymour was again using his whip on Silver Jet. Alec pulled Black Minx clear of the gray colt and urged her on with hands and feet and voice, forgetting completely that she had never responded to his urging before.

He didn't know which colts were stretched across the track and closest to him. Eclipse? Wintertime? Lone Hope? Olympus? Rampart? It didn't matter. The race was now in its final stage.

Just after the mile pole Black Minx had her nose at Silver Jet's saddle. But there she hung as Seymour got more speed from his tiring gray colt. The jockey never looked at Alec, nor Alec at him. Their heads were extended, close to their mounts and straining with them. Their eyes were only on the long-striding chestnut colt ahead.

Halfway down the stretch, Golden Vanity neared the mile-and-an-eighth pole. *Was the chestnut colt faltering?* Alec asked himself. Were his great strides becoming shorter? Certainly Silver Jet and his filly were not going any faster *yet they were pulling up on the chestnut leader*! Slowly at first, then even faster, even though Nino Nella was using hands and feet against his mount as though his very life depended upon it.

At the mile-and-an-eighth pole Golden Vanity quit with shocking suddenness. He quit as fast as he had been running before. He staggered and slowed, like a car out of gas. And nothing Nino Nella did could enable his colt to pick up stride again.

The pandemonium on either side of the track reached new

heights as the crowd became aware of the favorite's sudden collapse. Golden Vanity couldn't carry his blinding speed more than a mile and an eighth! He never had; Nino Nella had always kept him under wraps from the mile pole on, and he couldn't go the Derby distance! The spectators' frenzied eyes left the staggering chestnut, seeking the new champion in the field that was surging forward, closing in and engulfing the beaten favorite.

Alec had Black Minx's nose at Silver Jet's neck as they flashed past Golden Vanity. Alec's head was bobbing now as he tried desperately to get her in front of Silver Jet. Yet he felt certain that the race was over for him, and for Seymour too. They had stayed with Golden Vanity all during that terrible early pace. They had killed off the Derby favorite but they had destroyed themselves as well. Those behind—those riders who had saved their colts—would be coming on now, all-out in the final drive to the wire. Already there were heads stretched across the track from them, all so close, a neck behind but no more, and the finish line still so far away.

Less than a furlong to go, an eighth of a mile, just two hundred and twenty yards! But it seemed an endless distance, one of torture and strain, of heart and courage.

Alec didn't realize he was pumping his legs shockingly hard against Black Minx. He was not aware that she was actually *responding to his urging,* that she had done so all during the long-stretch run. He knew only that she was gaining on Silver Jet, that her nose was at the gray's head; *then* she was out in front! A hundred yards to go and there was no colt in front of them!

She was straining her utmost, trying to maintain her

speed, trying to respond again to his urging to keep on. She was running on heart alone.

The stands were one continuous shattering roar, and suddenly they became a screaming madhouse. Alec saw the white, pushing face on his right. *Eclipse! Watch Eclipse,* Henry had said. Watch him! Watch him! Watch him! *Oh, filly. More, more, more!* Head and head they bobbed as one. Eye and eye. She kept going. She never fell back. She took the challenge, met it, staved it off, and went on. She pushed her head in front of Eclipse. Now she was a neck ahead! The burly brown colt was beaten—with the wire less than twenty-five yards away.

*Courage. The greatest test of all is to repel challenges from behind.*

Henry's words flashed through Alec's brain as he saw the wire so close and Eclipse beaten. But he never got a chance to breathe, to think about winning. *A red-hooded head was far on the outside of the track.* A head that pushed relentlessly forward until it inched ahead of them with only a few strides to go. *Wintertime,* being moved by Billy Watts in the final surging sprint of a champion!

Alec let out a yell, strained forward, lifted, pleaded. And from deep within the black filly came a last response. She rallied, her muscles and heart gathering in one final effort. She won back the inches lost to Wintertime in those last few strides. Then she and the blood bay colt swept as one beneath the finish wire.

Alec collapsed in his saddle, his hands flat on the filly's wet, throbbing neck. He let her slow down as she pleased. He didn't know if she'd won. Neither did young Billy Watts on Wintertime, nor the screaming, shrieking thousands who had watched, nor the judges whose job it was to decide. The camera alone would give the answer, and the electric sign-board flashed the words PHOTO FINISH.

Alec knew only that his filly was as game as they come, *as game as her great sire.*

# "Anything Can Happen . . ."

## 22

Alec turned her around and came back with the others. But only Billy Watts and Wintertime stayed on the track with him and the filly to accept the tremendous ovation of the crowd. Neither rider approached the runway to the presentation stand where a small group, including the Governor of the state, was awaiting the winner of the Kentucky Derby.

Alec kept Black Minx in the middle of the track and away from the packed rails. The stands were quieting down. The screams that had risen with the mounting excitement of the race were over. There was a stunned silence. All eyes turned to the great board, where the number of the winner would be posted any second.

Billy Watts rode Wintertime in a circle, coming within a few feet of Alec. Watts's face was streaked with dirt that had been thrown up at him by front-running horses for a mile and a quarter. And no longer was it so boyish. Regardless of

236

the results of the race, he had become a hardened, experienced rider with a Derby behind him. And if his number 9 flashed on the board he would ride Wintertime into the circle, one of the youngest jockeys ever to win the classic.

He tried unsuccessfully to smile. "We knew we could beat the chestnut and the gray, but we didn't figure on your filly being up there," he said to Alec. "We raced just the way we'd planned except for you and the filly." His eyes left Alec for Black Minx, and he saw her bleeding leg. "She's hurt in the left fore. Did you know that?"

Quickly Alec leaned sideways in his saddle. He saw the dark-red stain with some blood still trickling from the wound. He could not tell how deep or how serious it was. She wasn't limping, for she was too tired to feel anything.

He couldn't dismount until the results were announced, and besides, he could do nothing for her while he remained on the track. Turning to the jam-packed rails, he looked for Henry. But it was a futile search. No one, not even Henry, could get through to him before the photograph of the finish was developed and the results were posted.

Suddenly he heard a deafening roar. Alec turned to the board. *Number 5 was on top!* It was over now, officially over, and Black Minx had managed to get her nose in front of Wintertime after all!

He rode toward the presentation stand, thinking of the many times he had criticized her for her lack of courage and will to win. And she had raced as she had with an injured leg!

Henry came down the runway and took hold of her bridle. Alec said, "She's hurt. It's the left fore."

"I know. I saw it happen at the gate when she ran into

Silver Jet. You didn't know." Henry looked down at the leg. "And she doesn't yet."

"We ought to get her right back to the vet," Alec said. He couldn't stand any long presentation ceremony now, knowing the filly was hurt.

Henry continued leading her toward the group awaiting them, toward the Gold Cup being held by the Governor, toward the television cameras and the waiting press, *toward the world*. "We're not going to cheat her out of this," he said. "She rates it as much as any Derby winner ever did. Maybe more. She broke the record, Alec. Did you know that? *She won in two minutes one second flat.*"

"You mean . . ." But Alec had no chance to say more. They were in the winner's circle and a blanket of roses was being placed about Black Minx's neck. Countless photographers were taking her picture, and the television cameras were on her as she stood quietly in the ring, almost posing, as if she knew full well the place she was taking in Kentucky Derby history.

Henry and Alec managed to keep their part in the ceremony as brief as possible. So it was only a short time later that they were back in the barn and the stable veterinarian was taking care of Black Minx.

The area outside the barn was roped off. The press, who had been deprived of their interviews by the short presentation ceremony, waited anxiously for the famous trainer and rider to leave the barn.

It was quiet in the stall. Neither Alec nor Henry mentioned the race. They only watched the doctor and waited. Black Minx had begun limping on the way back to the barn, and now was holding her toe off the straw bedding. Mingled with the smell of sweat and leather was the sharp odor of medication. A tub of hot water steamed beside the veterinarian while he worked, his hands in rubber gloves. Finally he bandaged her leg and stood up.

Alec was afraid to speak but Henry thrust out his jaw and asked, "How bad is it, Doc?"

"Not bad."

"How bad is that?" Henry persisted. The veterinarian was removing his gloves, putting them away. "Don't hedge on me, Doc. We've been friends too long for that."

The veterinarian's steady blue eyes were neither grave nor sad. "You always expect the worst, Henry, don't you?"

"Then I never get let down."

The veterinarian smiled. "I guess you're right, at that." He turned to the filly, putting his hand on her blanketed body. "You've still got a fine filly. She's all right, and it won't take long for her to heal and be . . ."

Alec felt his muscles go limp. He had been tense so long, and now . . . *now he could let go.* She was going to be all right. He went to her head, stroking it softly. He never heard Henry and the doctor as they left the stall.

Sometime later Henry appeared at the half-door. "Alec," he called. "Bring her over here. They want some head pictures of you two."

Alec turned her around. He wanted only to rest, to relax—and he was certain she did too. But this was part of it all; it wouldn't end until they left Churchill Downs.

The photographers took their pictures of Alec and the filly. They took pictures of Henry as he sat in the old canvas chair before the stall.

"Cross your knees and look sly," they told Henry. "Look

as if you knew all week that you had the Derby winner in your barn."

Henry smiled. "But I didn't," he said. "I'm as surprised as you are."

"We're not so surprised," they insisted.

While the pictures were being taken, Alec asked Henry, "How did the others finish?"

"Eclipse was up behind Wintertime. Silver Jet was fourth, then came Long Hope, Break-up . . ."

"But Golden Vanity?" Alec interrupted.

"I'm coming to him. Olympus finished three lengths behind Break-up. Then came Golden Vanity and last of all, Rampart."

"Boy, Golden Vanity must have stopped cold in that last furlong."

"He certainly did," a reporter told him. "He broke every record from the half to a mile and an eighth. Then he was so burned out he finished in a cakewalk. We had a feeling all along he couldn't go a mile and a quarter."

*Sure,* Alec thought, *you knew it all along.* Before the Derby they were acclaiming Golden Vanity as the greatest colt of all time. Now they were disowning him. *How fleeting can fame be?*

The reporters had turned to Henry again. "What do you plan to do with that big purse, Henry?"

From his chair Henry looked up at Alec. "We'll be buying some more mares, among other things," he answered. "Hopeful Farm is on its way."

The press turned to look at Black Minx. "Will you race her in the Preakness and Belmont Stakes? A filly's never won the Triple Crown, you know."

"I can't answer that," Henry replied. "It depends upon how fast her leg heals and how things look to us. We're not thinking about the Triple Crown now. We got the *big one* today, and that's all that matters."

"Yes," they agreed, "it's all that matters. We're going to say in our papers that never before have we seen such great heart and courage as Black Minx displayed today by holding herself together and turning back Eclipse and then Wintertime in those last few strides . . . and all with a bad leg. Will you like that, Henry?"

"You couldn't put it better, boys. I like that very much, and she deserves every good thing you have to say about her."

They turned to Alec. "Do you have any last comment to make, Alec? When did you know you had the race won?"

"I didn't know," Alec said. "Not until our number went up on the board."

"Do you have anything to say about a filly winning the Derby?" they asked. "It's happened only once before—and never in such record-breaking time, of course."

"Just that *anything can happen in the Derby*," Alec answered.

They scowled, disappointed and in need of a better comment for their papers. "But that's been said before."

Alec smiled. "I know. You're the ones who've said it. You knew it all the time."

The filly blew out her nostrils, snorting, as though to add emphasis to his remark. He touched her head and she snorted again.

Henry got to his feet. "That's all, boys. The Derby's over for another year."

They were alone again, just the three of them in the stall. Alec stood at Black Minx's side and Henry in front of her. The old trainer put his hand in his pocket and withdrew a carrot. He offered it to her.

Alec smiled. "You told me never to do that. You said no hand-feeding, ever."

Henry's eyes never left Black Minx. "It's different this time," he said softly. "This is the exception to the rule."

For a moment the filly only sniffed the carrot, her eyes leaving it to look puzzledly at Henry. Then she looked at it again. Finally she took it.

Alec asked, "Do you have any more?"

Henry nodded and put a carrot in Alec's hand.

Alec offered it to her, and she took the carrot more readily this time. "I've waited a long while to do that," he said.

Henry straightened her forelock, then stroked her head. "You did it," he told her. "You really did. You're the gamest filly, the best little filly in the whole wide world."

Alec's hand moved lovingly across her neck. "She's that, all right, Henry. She sure is."

Black Minx didn't move. She seemed to know what this was all about. She accepted their offerings, their embraces, in a very queenly way. Her manner indicated that she was getting only what was long due her, and that she had known all along no colt would beat her in the Kentucky Derby.

Perhaps she had known. Alec and Henry wouldn't have been surprised. She was that kind of girl.

# ABOUT THE AUTHOR

Walter Farley's love for horses began when he was a small boy living in Syracuse, New York, and continued as he grew up in New York City, where his family moved. Unlike most city children, he was able to fulfill this love through an uncle who was a professional horseman. Young Walter spent much of his time with this uncle, learning about the different kinds of horse training and the people associated with each.

Walter Farley began to write his first book, *The Black Stallion,* while he was a student at Brooklyn's Erasmus Hall High School and Mercersburg Academy in Pennsylvania. He finished it and had it published while he was still an undergraduate at Columbia University.

The appearance of *The Black Stallion* brought such an enthusiastic response from young readers that Mr. Farley went on to write more stories about the Black, and about other horses as well. He now has twenty-five books to his credit, including his first dog story, *The Great Dane Thor,* and his story of America's greatest thoroughbred, *Man O' War.* His books have been enormously successful in this country, and have also been published in fourteen foreign countries.

When not traveling, Walter Farley and his wife, Rosemary, divide their time between a farm in Pennsylvania and a beach house in Florida.